THE
GOLDEN PIG

GOLDEN PIG

THE
GOLDEN PIG

10 APR 2012

NORTH HARROW LIBRARY
429-433 PINNER ROAD
NORTH HARROW
HARROW HA1 4HN
TEL: 020 8427 0611

THE PENNY BROTHERS

Copyright © 2012 Mark and Jonathan Penny

The moral rights of the authors have been asserted.

First published in 2009 by Lightning Press
20 Hollywell Road, Knowle, Solihull, West Midlands, B93 9JY

Apart from any fair dealing for the purposes of research or private study, or criticism or review, as permitted under the Copyright, Designs and Patents Act 1988, this publication may only be reproduced, stored or transmitted, in any form or by any means, with the prior permission in writing of the publishers, or in the case of reprographic reproduction in accordance with the terms of licences issued by the Copyright Licensing Agency. Enquiries concerning reproduction outside those terms should be sent to the publishers.

All characters appearing in this work are fictitious.
Any resemblance to real persons, living or dead, is purely coincidental.

Matador
9 Priory Business Park
Kibworth Beauchamp
Leicestershire LE8 0RX, UK
Tel: (+44) 116 279 2299
Fax: (+44) 116 279 2277
Email: books@troubador.co.uk
Web: www.troubador.co.uk/matador

ISBN 978 1780880 679

British Library Cataloguing in Publication Data.
A catalogue record for this book is available from the British Library.
Printed and bound in the UK by TJ Internatioanl, Padstow, Cornwall

Matador is an imprint of Troubador Publishing Ltd

MIX
Paper from
responsible sources
FSC
www.fsc.org   FSC® C013056

Authors' Note

It may be wondered why this book is divided into "parts" instead of chapters. The answer gives some small insight into how the book came into being in the first place. It all began, more years ago than we care to remember, as a game of sibling rivalry to see which of us could create the most exciting and outrageous plotlines, the most believable yet quirky characters and the funniest dialogue and gags. We took it in turns to write a part then, when inspiration had deserted us, posted the story so far to the other to add the next part. Only when the book was complete did we review the manuscript to iron out the numerous inconsistencies, dead-ends and longuers. Thus the structure had, and still retains, a meaning for us that chapters never could.

The Penny Brothers, January 2009

HARROW LIBRARIES	
01693488	
Bertrams	22/02/2012
CRI	£7.99

Part One

Hymie Goldman was a detective of no fixed abode, hairstyle, or opinions; they all came and went like the north wind. Unlike his name, he wasn't Jewish; the closest he'd ever come to Judaism was walking past a synagogue in Golders Green. His real name was Artie Shaw, after the once famous but now deceased jazz clarinettist. As dead musicians weren't noted for their investigative skills, and he was frequently skating on the thin ice of bankruptcy, he'd begun changing his name in a futile attempt to attract new clients and repel old creditors. It had worked in reverse and he was now on his third identity. At least it gave him the chance to advertise himself as "under new management" from time to time.

His last incarnation, as Jackson Pollock, man of mystery, had been selected by sticking a pin in an encyclopaedia of modern art he'd picked up at a car-boot sale. He should have foreseen its cockney rhyming-slang potential, but he frequently missed the blatantly obvious. The irony of choosing the name of a dead artist over that of a dead musician was entirely lost on him.

He had never felt like a *real* detective; probably because he'd trained as an electrician. After his father died under the wheels of a bus, caught taking photographs of an unfaithful husband, in the nightclub Flagrante Delicto, he found himself running the family firm. He had tried to sell it, of course, but nobody wanted it.

B Shaw, Private Investigators: it was corny but catchy; much like the old man himself. He'd re-branded it "JP Confidential; no case too large or small" in the Pollock era, and invested blood, sweat and tears, not to mention his last penny in a sensational new website. He'd hoped it would bring in a tsunami of new business, but he was still waiting on the beach. His father, who'd had a saying for every occasion, had always told him, "Life's a beach, and then you die." He had studiously avoided the seaside ever since.

Everything about Goldman was a twenty-five carat fake: in his thirty-eight years on the planet he had pretended to be so many things to so many people that he scarcely knew who he was any longer. His flat had been repossessed so many times that he kept a suitcase by the front door. Having recently been evicted, he now lived in his office, contrary to the terms of the lease. Most of his meagre belongings had to be hidden from the bailiffs when he wasn't actually using them, and even the clothes he stood up in bore the hallmark of the charity shop; a cut that didn't flatter and a style that was last fashionable in 1986.

Work had been thin on the ground of late, which suited his temperament, if not his desire to eat regularly. On the morning of 4th July he awoke, slumped across his desk, after another fitful night's sleep in the swivel chair.

Bleary-eyed, he surveyed his kingdom at 792A Finchley Road with the haunted look of one waking from a dream of paradise, to find he had taken the wrong turn at the last roundabout and ended up in hell. Even in his dreams he should have known better than to buy a satnav from Dodgy Dave down the King's Head.

He stood up, stretched and farted. It helped him to limber up. He even made a valiant attempt to touch his toes, but he had been a stranger to exercise for so long that his body rejected the challenge: his toes remained distant and unattainable, while he descended into a fit of giddiness that caused him to head-butt a passing wall.

"Ouch!"

Returning to the vertical, he peered through the blinds to make sure he was alone before lifting the loose floorboard beneath his desk with an old screwdriver. He retrieved his laptop, logged on and checked his inbox. On quiet days he spent hours fiddling with his laptop. However, since *Reader's*

Digest had developed a way of tracking him in hyperspace and he didn't need any more free business cards, he hurriedly logged off again. He completed his ablutions in his usual peremptory fashion and breakfasted on the remains of a packet of cornflakes and some long-life milk, which was nearing retirement.

Downstairs the Black Kat café was just opening up, and on the mean streets of Finchley anarchy and chaos were pitching their stall for the day.

An insistent burst of wood-splintering knocking sliced through the fug in his brain.

"There's no one here but the cleaners," he croaked, trying to sound like an old crone.

He had just covered his laptop with an old copy of the *Sun* when the door flew open to reveal Janis, a world-weary seventeen-year-old he had recruited after that unfortunate incident involving, in no particular order, surveillance, beauty queens in Notting Hill, and his arrest for kerb-crawling. It had all been a ridiculous joke by some Jamaican taxi driver of doubtful paternity, but the police had been highly suspicious of him for months afterwards.

In retrospect, he could see how it might help an investigator following women around for a living to be female, so he hired Janis.

He liked to refer to Janis as his apprentice, as though he had some higher level of knowledge to impart, and she was a dedicated student of the craft of investigation. In truth, he was still learning the job himself and she was employed on a government training scheme, if you could call poverty wages and brain-death work training.

"What did you say about the cleaners?" asked Janis, binning the last of the junk mail she'd retrieved from their letterbox.

"I said it's disgusting in here; just wait till I see those cleaners."

"I expect they'd be glad to see *you*. I can't remember the last time you paid them."

"Yes, well, I can't sit here all day discussing the decline

of the great British cleaner; why don't you pop out and get us two coffees?"

"The Black Kat?" she queried.

"Unfortunately that's all there is, Jan. Perhaps one day there will be coffee shops on every corner where the coffee is actually drinkable, but for now, needs must. Oh, and get a couple of slices of toast while you're at it."

He ushered her away with an imperious wave of his hand.

"Is there anything in petty cash?"

"Unless you count the pawn tickets, I fear not."

He sighed like a deflating beach ball. The only appointment in his diary was with Barnet County Bailiffs. They were dropping by to collect what was left of his office furniture. Where were his clients going to sit? The question was largely academic as they were increasingly an endangered species. It was all very well saying "it's not over until the fat lady sings" but now that that pneumatic young opera singer from Cardiff had moved in next door, he was beginning to feel like an extra from *Turandot*.

As the familiar strains of "Nessun dorma" drifted through his keyhole, the green, plastic, retro-styled telephone on his desk began to trill. It was probably the Indian call-centre again, or the double-glazing salesman with the stammer, or that drug-crazed loony who just yelled a string of random numbers down the phone at him, then rang off.

"Twenty-four, thirty-six, forty-two, don't be late!"

What could it mean? Was it the vital statistics of the girl in the "before" photo at the slimming club or just a series of menu items from the local Chinese takeaway? Special fried rice, sweet and sour pork balls or egg and chips in a black bean sauce perhaps? Ah well, that was the price you paid for advertising in *Catering World*. Still, it *was* cheaper than *Yellow Pages*.

Janis returned with a cup of the black sludge sold as coffee to the regulars of the Black Kat and a small bottle of still water. Her complexion had improved dramatically since she'd stopped drinking the coffee. Still, what choice did *he* have? Without caffeine he'd have to face the world as it really was:

scary. He couldn't even brew his own sludge now that the kettle too had finally succumbed to repossession.

"No toast, Jan?" He looked like a small child who had just been robbed of his bag of sweets.

"Their toaster's on the blink. It only does cremation."

"Unbelievable."

"I know. Mr Goldman, your phone's ringing."

Janis chivvied him, as ever, in her most apologetic tone. It wasn't his fault he was a complete halfwit; he was a man.

"Go and catch up with your filing," he snapped, peevishly.

His last resort was always to the absurd; since they hadn't had a client in weeks, there *was* no filing. Perhaps he meant her nails.

"It's all up to date," Janis said.

"Well, go and play with the paperclips."

She smiled her *patient* smile and retrieved the *Hendon and Finchley Times* from her designer shoulder bag. He lifted the phone to his ear as if he half expected it to bite.

"JP Confidential, no case too large...I'm sorry to have kept you, how may we help?"

"How *confidential* are you?"

"Oh great! Loonies!" he thought. He fought back the urge to drop the receiver, to scream obscenities into the mouthpiece, to ask "How long is a piece of string?" and settled for humility.

"They don't come any more confidential, madam," he said. "I personally guarantee to take all my clients' secrets to the grave."

"*Whose* grave?"

"Anyone you care to mention."

"Who are you? The owner?"

"Yes, Hymie Goldman."

"Are you Jewish?"

"Is the pope Catholic? Look, I'm a busy man; do you need a detective or a telephone chat line?"

"I may have a job for you. Meet me tonight and I'll tell you what I want you to do."

"Sure. As long as it's... ." He was going to say "legal" but thought better of it. Surely rejecting a case for purely *legal* reasons was unethical.

"As long as it's what?" she queried.

"It will keep till we meet, lady. When and where did you have in mind?" he asked.

"Eleven sharp at Ritzy's nightclub. You know it, I presume? Let's say the Glitter Lounge...no, better make it outside." She didn't want to be seen with him and she hadn't even met him. He had always been a fast worker, he reflected ruefully.

"Certainly, but how will I know you?" he continued.

"Don't worry, I'll find you."

The line died.

Hymie was already fantasising about fat fees and how he was going to spend them, when the doorbell rang downstairs, shattering his reverie.

"Your nine-thirty is here, Mr Goldman," announced Janis, efficiently.

"Who or what is a *nine-thirty*, Jan?" he responded with vague bemusement.

"Why, an appointment, of course."

"Are you sure? An *appointment*? But the bailiffs aren't due until later. Who's it with?"

"A lady called Sarah Chandar."

"Sorry, Jan, she means nothing to me. Have I ever met her?"

"She seemed to know you. She said she'd seen the website and was most impressed. She said she could help us grow the business, so I thought that as your diary was fairly free, you might as well listen to what she had to say."

He pondered. "Thank you, Janis, I know you mean well, but next time, please discuss it with me first. I may have had an important meeting planned."

"Yeah, right," she thought, and only said, "Yes, of course, Mr Goldman." She remained the consummate professional, even if she was working for a rank amateur.

Janis pressed a button on her switchboard, triggering the door release, and invited their visitor to join them.

"Hello, you must be Mr Goldman. I'm Sarah Chandar from Ceefer Capital. It's good of you to see me."

She was Indian, maybe thirty years old, pretty but forbiddingly professional and polished in her manner, like the younger daughter of a millionaire industrialist.

"Not at all, Sarah, I'm glad I could fit you into my busy schedule," lied the man from Finchley, as Janis hovered attentively at the door.

"Please, have a seat. Can I offer you a drink?" He was determined to maintain the illusion that this was a *real* business.

"Oh, just a still water, please."

Janis eyed her bottle of water with regret before twisting off the cap, pouring it into the office glass and proffering it to their guest.

"Thanks, Jan," he said, as she left his office.

"I expect you're wondering what I'm doing here, Mr Goldman?"

"Yes," he thought. "Not at all," he said. "It's always a pleasure to network with the wider business community. You never know, one day you may be coming to see me as a client. Am I right?"

"Exactly, Mr Goldman, you are clearly a shrewd businessman. I knew you would be."

"Thank you." She seemed harmless enough, but he couldn't help wondering what she wanted. Surely not money?

"Which is why I won't beat about the bush any longer."

"I'm afraid I make it a habit never to contribute to…"

"I'd like to buy a stake in your business."

"Ahem," said Hymie, choking in surprise.

Life never ceased to amaze him. Just when you thought it was all over; that there was nothing left to play for, the game of chance was at its most dangerous. Who would have thought it? People wanted to give him money. It was priceless. It was plainly ludicrous.

"What interests you in JP Confidential, Sarah?" he said at last, as though it were the most natural question in the world.

"Its potential, Mr Goldman."

"Oh yes, we have plenty of that," he said, smiling to himself. Potential was the flipside of what he generally called problems.

"I have examined your website in some detail, and have to say it is one of the best I have ever seen. Your case histories are almost too good to be true, you are looking to the future and you appear to have a strong brand. With a backer like Ceefer Capital you could turn "JP Confidential, no case too large or small" into a world-class business."

"How much of the business do you want then, ten per cent? Twenty?"

She smiled for the first time. It belied the earnestness in her face.

"All of it, of course, Mr Goldman. We would, naturally enough, incentivise you to stay on."

There was always a catch.

"And how much will you pay me for it, Sarah?"

He found it difficult to suppress his mounting excitement. Could it be real? Or was he being set up for some new TV reality show where she would either offer him millions, only to pull the rug out from under him and leave him looking like a credulous berk, or offer him the fifty pence it was really worth, to uproarious laughter from a studio audience?

"It depends on your trading performance, business plan and cash-flow projections, but perhaps as much as half a million."

He had begun to glaze over when the "m" word revived him with a start.

"Pounds sterling?" he asked deliriously.

Yet, even as his conscious mind was rapidly descending into euphoria, some nagging doubt at the back of it wouldn't quite let him be. Outside his flimsy office walls, the real world was clamouring to get in.

The heavy tread of size-twelve boots on the stairs heralded the arrival of two burly six-footers in ill-fitting suits. They pushed past Janis with her outraged protestations but hesitated on the threshold of his inner sanctum, unaccustomed to seeing him in a business meeting. They glowered through the glass at him.

It was all the opportunity he needed.

"I was afraid of this, Sarah. Some business rivals have been showing a keen interest in JP Confidential of late and they must have got wind that other bidders of your calibre were making overtures. Rather than have you facing any unpleasantness, perhaps we can adjourn this meeting for the time being. I promise I won't do anything rash until I have had a chance to consider your offer. You have my office number, but here's my mobile number just in case." He handed her a card.

Before she even knew what was happening, Ms Chandar found herself whisked out of her chair and politely but firmly shown the door. The last words she heard as she descended the staircase were Goldman's entreaties to his "business rivals" not to broadcast their latest offer to HM Revenue and Customs. She supposed he meant herself. He was clearly a tricky customer to do business with.

The bailiffs seemed to be enjoying the cabaret, but were reluctant to drop their guard, having been left in the lurch so often before. Goldman regularly claimed to have suffered a family bereavement or to be traumatised by a terminal illness, and they suspected that it was only a matter of time before he would claim insanity. Although it was increasingly uncertain whether he had anything worth lying about, old habits died hard. They marched into his newly vacated office and started eying up the contents of the room, with a view to a quick sale, Janis following at their heels like a terrier.

Having seen off his guest with his usual old-world charm, Hymie sauntered back to his office with little evident pleasure.

"I did ask them to wait, Mr Goldman."

"It's okay, Jan, it's only a social call; there's nothing left for them to take. So, what can I do for you two plug-uglies?"

They stood in the doorway like two gorillas on day release, knuckles dusting the lino.

"You know the procedure, Goldman; we hand you the warrant, you make a big song and dance about it, and then we walk off into the sunset with whatever we can find. Usually zippo. Can't we just cut to the chase today? I have a lunch date," said the burlier bailiff, with the joined-up eyebrows.

"Say, maybe *you'd* like to buy a stake in the business too?" suggested Hymie, chirpily.

"He has me in stitches. Buy a stake in *your* business? Do we look like we've just escaped from the zoo?" asked the second bailiff.

"Well, now you come to mention it..."

"Button it, Goldman," they snapped, in unison.

"But seriously, gents, I do have *something* of value."

"On the level?" they enquired reluctantly, like dupes invited onstage by a magician.

"Certainly on the level," added Hymie, as his strategy miraculously dropped into place.

"But is it worth hard cash?" persisted Harry, the burlier one.

"Oh, bundles of it. You take my advice; put your shirt on Devil May Care in the 12.10 at Uttoxeter. It can't lose."

The other bailiff, Larry, reached into his coat pocket. Hymie was half expecting him to produce a banana, but he merely retrieved the usual paperwork and thrust it insistently on him with the practised ease of a man used to giving bad news. He would have made a good politician, thought Hymie.

"Seriously though, gents," he added, "if the horse doesn't win, I'll be a Dutchman's uncle." Those ruddy bailiffs had been taking away his stuff for years, it was about time they lost *their* shirts, he thought.

Larry, who evidently thought that *any* tip was worth backing, if only each way, retrieved a notebook from his other pocket and scrawled down the name of the horse in large infantile handwriting, while his colleague, Harry, simply looked on with disdain.

"It was a tip from inside the stable," said Hymie.

"Who from, the horse's mother?" responded Harry, sardonically.

"It was at twenty to one last night, surely that's worth giving my premises a miss for a few weeks? I know you gents seem to have a problem believing me, but I was actually in negotiations to offload, ahem, to *sell* the business when you came barging in."

"Well, you're right there, mate," resumed Harry. "It's easy to tell when you're lying: your lips are moving."

"Nice one, Harry," added Larry, somewhat redundantly.

"Okay, *Mr* Goldman, go on, how much was the Indian princess offering for your business empire? Don't tell me...all the jewels of the orient...or, say, fifty pence?"

"Put it this way, enough to allow me to retire to the country."

"Which one? Bangladesh?"

"How much do you want, anyway?" asked Goldman, irritated. "A tenner? Twenty quid?"

"No, mate, try £5,000 in unpaid rent," said Larry.

"What, for *this* flea pit? Would *you* pay it, gents?"

"That's neither here nor there, is it, Goldman?" said Harry. "You see, *you* signed the lease, not us. It beats me how someone called Goldman can be such a worthless tick."

Hymie reached into his back pocket for a dog-eared chequebook.

"Will you take a cheque, lads?"

They smiled. "Not in a million years, mate. We've got enough meaningless paperwork as it is; we're part of the EU paper mountain scheme," observed Harry, regretfully.

"Fine. I'd like to say it's been a pleasure doing business with you, but I'd be lying. Help yourselves; you're welcome to anything you can find, but I'll tell you now, the only things not on hire purchase are the collection of stress-relief toys, the fake marble ashtray, and Janis."

"You can prove that, I dare say?"

"I dare say," smirked Hymie. "Sadly, I have pressing business to attend to elsewhere. So, if you'll excuse me, gentlemen, I'll leave you in the capable hands of my apprentice, Miss Turner."

He winked conspiratorially at Janis, grabbed his army-surplus trench coat from the stand in the corner of his office, and headed for the congested streets of North London.

"Don't forget, guys, Devil May Care in the 12.10 at Uttoxeter. If you hurry, you may just catch it."

"You'll catch it one of these days, Goldman!" called Harry, after Hymie's retreating back.

Part Two

It was midday by the time he arrived at the park. He'd had to walk, owing to the increasing unreliability of his car. Just after he acquired the car phone he'd spilt hot coffee into the CD player, while overtaking on a hairpin bend, and driven through a hedge. Fortunately, no one had been injured and he'd managed to borrow the money to spring his car from the local garage, but it had never been quite the same.

"Here ducks! Here ducky ducky! Here ducks!"

He threw a low-carb, high-fibre Atkins bagel into the centre of a small gang of ducks, rendering one or two unconscious. He often visited the park, finding it cheap, therapeutic and a good way of killing time between cases. By now he knew every blade of grass in the place.

Eventually he managed to find a bench that was both dry and free from obscene graffiti – no small task in London. He sat and gazed across the vast expanse of mud and dog turds that aspired to be a football pitch. The posts had been used for spare fuel last Bonfire Night and no one had played there since the Barnet Bulldogs were decimated by a drug-dealer's Dobermanns.

Hours passed as he paced the footpath, trying to come up with a foolproof plan for selling the business to Ceefer Capital. If only *one* of the cases he had made up on the website had been true, he'd be home and dry. As it was, he would probably have to *solve* an investigation before they would take him seriously. No one went around giving out half a million quid for a nice website, surely? He would also need to get some *accounts* from somewhere; whatever *they* were. What had she asked him for? Cash-flow forecasts? His cash had been flowing out for years and he could hardly bring himself to read anything from the bank any longer. Clearly, he would have to be economical with the truth for a while longer.

Ritzy's was the kind of nightclub that used to stand on the corner of every main street in every decent-sized town in the 1970s; grotty and crying out for demolition on the outside, tacky and full of kitsch on the inside. The local council had left it standing to avoid having to erect slums or whatever social housing project their planning department was championing that month. Even slums cost money.

Hanging around outside in the pouring dark, he felt purple: marooned in the urban jungle; too scruffy, disillusioned and old either to fit in or care less. He pulled up the collar of his coat, unfolded the *Evening Standard*, which he had retrieved from the bin in the park, and settled down to wait. He turned to the horoscopes page and looked up his stars; 31st March, Aries: "Beware blonde bombshells bearing gifts, they are not all they seem. Sunny spells later." It must be that new astro-meteorologist.

He flipped through the remaining pages until he caught sight of something in the racing results. "Well, of all the...Devil May Care won by a head; those jammy b...ailiffs!"

Suddenly a taxi pulled up at the kerb and a vision of loveliness emerged, paid off the driver, and sashayed across the pavement towards him. To call her stunning would have been to cheapen the word; tall, blonde and drop-dead gorgeous with an hourglass figure and a smile that would stop a man dead in his tracks at a hundred paces. She didn't even have to begin to try to impress Goldman.

"You must be the detective," she said, her voice as smooth as velvet.

"Ye...ye...yes, Gymie Holdman," he yammered. He had never been a success with women, but like most men never gave up hope.

"Follow me."

To the ends of the earth, of course, but he was dreaming, surely? She led him around the corner to a parking lot, opened up an immaculate black Porsche and they sped off into the encroaching night.

"I didn't catch your name," he said, fidgeting nervously with his seat belt.

"I didn't throw it at you, but it's Lucretia, or rather Lucy...Lucy Scarlatti."

A strange name, probably an alias, but by now he was already along for the ride.

Her manner was brusque and businesslike. Nothing more was said as they screeched through a myriad of back streets, finally arriving at journey's end, a newly refurbished warehouse conversion. Once inside she became more communicative.

"Take a seat. Would you like a drink?"

"I'd rather hear about the job first."

"So sit down."

He sat.

"It's a family matter really. It all began with the death of my father a month or so ago..."

"I'm sorry to hear... ." It seemed the only thing to say.

"Don't be, he was a terrible man. When he died there was nothing left...nothing but debts...and the statuette. You might almost call it a family heirloom; a golden statuette of a pig."

"Is it worth much?" asked Hymie.

"It's mainly of sentimental value."

"That much!" he thought.

"In his youth my father travelled the world with the merchant navy. I think he bought the figurine in the Far East; China or Japan."

"Where do I come in?"

Hymie was getting the distinct impression that this was yet another case for his "unsolvables" file. The file couldn't have been much thicker had he been investigating the *Mary Celeste*, the abominable snowman and life on Mars.

"Under the will he left me everything. My sister, Steffie, doesn't even get a mention."

"And your sister has the pig, right?"

"Yes, the bitch! She's always been jealous of my success in lingerie modelling, so she persuaded one of her lovers to steal it. Can you get it back for me?"

"Why not call in the police?" he asked.

"As I said, it's a family matter."

"It could get messy," he said. He didn't like the sound of it, but needed the money.

She sized him up and took the measure of him in a glance. "A hundred pounds a day, plus expenses?" she suggested.

"When do I start?" asked Hymie, resisting the urge to add "How about last Tuesday!"

Lucy left the room briefly, returning with a thousand pounds in used notes. "I'll expect a phone call every few days and a full progress report each week," she said. "Hopefully, you should have something concrete within the week."

"As long as it's not an overcoat," he thought.

She passed him a page from a notebook with a handwritten address scribbled on it and her business card.

"Those are her last known address and contact numbers. There's a photo of the pig attached. Call me."

"Certainly. Now, about that drink?"

"Maybe some other time. Find my pig, Mr Goldman."

It was a long walk back to 792A Finchley Road, but time flies when you've got a grand burning a hole in your pocket. His only regret was not having had the presence of mind to ask for a larger advance, but he had simply been struck dumb at the sight of so much hard cash. It would have been churlish or foolhardy to quibble with a woman so clearly used to getting her own way.

Back at the office everything had gone AWOL except the telephone and the hot-oil stress-relief lamp. How a lamp could relieve stress had never been adequately explained to him, but he'd always liked day-glo orange, and since he'd bought it with the proceeds of his first case he couldn't bring himself to part with it. The bailiffs had dismissed it as worthless junk, which it was.

He rang for a pizza; the biggest, with extra everything.

Only when his stomach was full could he think at all clearly.

Leaning against the windowsill he gazed out into the empty street below. "Benny's Unbeatable Bakery" flashed in neon lights from the opposite side of the Finchley Road. Benny had been baking the best pizzas in North London for longer than Hymie could remember, maybe a year even.

The phone rang from its new home on the floor of his office. It was partially illuminated by the garish orange glimmer of the lamp and cast a distorted shadow on the wall. He wondered who could be calling at this time of night. Some desperate, friendless character, that was for sure. He lifted the receiver.

"Hello, Mr Goldman, it's Sarah Chandar calling."

"Oh, yes, of course. How are you, Sarah? I was sorry you had to leave so suddenly."

"Fine, thanks...but you *asked* me to leave, don't you remember?"

"Yes, it was essential. I couldn't risk your safety with those two thugs on the loose."

"Who were they?"

"Just a couple of longstanding business rivals: hardened, cynical men operating beyond the outer fringes of the law; men who would stop at nothing to get my business. After you left, they tried to make me an offer I couldn't refuse."

"So, what happened?" she asked, in a breathless whisper.

"I declined, of course. After all, hadn't I just promised you first refusal?"

"Yes, but I thought you were just bluffing to drive the price up."

He fell silent, as though he had been mortally offended and could no longer find the strength to continue with the conversation. It worked a treat.

"I'm sorry, Mr Goldman. Can we meet to talk over my ideas for the business?"

"We can meet, but with a business *this* good, you can't afford to hang around. I'm not going to change anything until we've reached a deal on the price.

I believe you said JP Confidential was worth around a

million pounds and that's my price," bluffed Hymie, the tough negotiator.

"I said half a million," Sarah corrected him, "and even that depends on the satisfactory completion of due diligence."

She might just as well have been speaking Greek.

"You can do all the diligence you like, but the price is a million quid. Take it or leave it."

She left it.

"Sarah? Sarah? Let's not be hasty. How about nine-fifty?" He was talking to himself.

She'd be back, of course; businesses like JP Confidential didn't grow on trees.

Part Three

64 Rotten Park Road looked like any other '50s semi. The district was fairly affluent, indeed it had been tipped as "up and coming" by the local firm of estate agents, Brown, Darling and McHaggis, if you could believe a word they said.

Unbeknown to many, number 64 was the home of a premier-league sleuth, the detective giant of the Metropolitan Constabulary, Inspector Ray Decca. The fact that he rarely set foot in the place was more a reflection of his dedication to duty than to any disaffection with the neighbourhood, though having a wife who could have nagged for Britain may have tilted the scales in favour of the police station.

Promotion had come quickly and easily to him; easier still after he'd joined the secret Mahjong Society. So what if he'd had to swear allegiance to the Mighty Jong while wearing a traffic cone on his head with his left trouser leg rolled up to the knee? It was all part of the rich tapestry of police life.

That night he and his wife sat up reading in bed. Decca's book was a detective novel by Simenon. In fact it was lying open in his hands at page fifty-three, where it had stubbornly remained since last Thursday. It wasn't so much that page fifty-three was particularly brilliant or exciting; simply that

Decca's mind was elsewhere. Sometimes he was on the verge of solving a major case and being congratulated by the Chief Constable, at other times, such as after a particularly bad day, he was spending his early retirement on a sun-kissed beach in the South Pacific, surrounded by dusky maidens in little grass skirts with large coconuts.

Mrs Decca, or Sheila as she was known among her friends at the Women's Institute, was gently nagging in the background as Decca's mind raced across the globe to paradise.

"Did you pay my car insurance like you promised, Ray?"

"Hmmmmmm…"

"Is that hmmm yes or hmmm no?"

"Hmmmmmm?"

"You're not paying attention to me, Raymond!"

She always called him Raymond when she was working up to a really big nag.

"Sorry, dear…?"

"My car insurance?"

"Yes, dear, it's all sorted."

"Did you remember to book a table at La Bistro? You haven't forgotten it's our anniversary next week, now have you?"

"Hmmmmmm…"

"Don't bother! There's something I've been meaning to tell you for some time…"

"Hmmmmmm, yes dear."

"I'm leaving you. I've found someone else; someone who appreciates me!"

"Hmmmmmm, that's nice, dear."

"You're not listening to a word, are you, Ray?"

"Hmmmmmm, yes dear…I mean, no dear. What did you say?"

"Why don't you just get the hell back to the office?!"

"Hmmmmmm?"

A few short minutes later the sound of raised voices, followed by breaking furniture could be heard from number 64. A dishevelled man in a Crombie overcoat appeared at the front door. Closing it behind him he climbed into the driver's seat of the blue Ford Mondeo in the driveway, revved the engine in a belated gesture of defiance, and drove away. Net curtains were twitching all along the road. The Neighbourhood Watch Committee would have something to say about this.

Part Four

A shaft of light illuminated the cracked lino. The noise from the street below was deafening. Janis had phoned, to confirm, what he already knew, that the bailiffs had taken his remaining furniture. Hymie told her to take the day off. He could be generous to a fault, when it didn't matter.

He sat on the floor of his office, wondering whether there was any point in buying more furniture for the bailiffs to repossess. He tried to lift the loose floorboard to see if he still had a laptop, but his screwdriver had been in the drawer of the desk the bailiffs had taken and his fingernails were too chewed to get any grip. The best ruddy website in the whole investigations universe and he couldn't get onto a computer to see if he had any enquiries! What kind of a tin-pot firm was he running? He shrugged and stood up; it didn't do to dwell on things he couldn't change.

"Up and at 'em, H, there's work to be done!" exclaimed Hymie.

He often talked to himself. It had become a bad habit, a legacy from childhood days when imaginary friends had brought him some kind of comfort. These days he didn't even know he was doing it.

He enjoyed being his own boss and loved working as a detective, but he had a talent for failure and knew deep down that he would never be rich. Even the prospect of an Indian venture capitalist, with an open chequebook, couldn't dispel the fear that whatever happened he would lose.

Despite this he was a survivor. He fleeced the occasional

punter for as much as his conscience would allow and wrote frequent grovelling letters to his bank manager – Tony Talbot from the bank that liked to say yes, except to him.

In his rented lock-up at the back of the alley he climbed into the driver's seat of his Zebaguchi 650; a five-litre gas-guzzling fuel-injected monstrosity that belonged in a prehistoric automobile museum and had long since eaten him out of house and home. It looked like an early prototype of a De Lorean and drove like a Chieftain tank.

He switched on the VDU. Lights flickered on the console. Encouraged, he typed in the ignition code, and presto! music drifted from the left-hand speaker.

"Nessun flippin' dorma!" he cursed, switching off the radio.

He flicked the transmission switch and turned over the engine. At the third splutter an explosion erupted from the twin chrome exhausts and the car lurched forward belching smoke and flames. Now *that* was something like a car.

After a cursory glance at the scrap of paper provided by his client, he put his foot to the floor. Four bald tyres spun on wet Tarmac and the rust-riddled dream machine careened down the street in a cloud of purple smoke.

An hour later, Hymie Goldman, private investigator, pulled up outside a quaint olde worlde cottage in South Mimms. It seemed quiet enough, but you could never be sure. He parked round a nearby corner, a few hundred metres away, then retraced his steps on foot. Approaching the front door with studied indifference, he rang the bell and waited.

Nothing.

His plan was to avoid climbing through any windows. He would fill in the details as he went along, but first he would have to get inside the house using some plausible cover story. His name was John, a gas-meter-reader from Enfield. He rang the bell a second time and a third, beginning to imagine himself in the part; he was married with two kids, who attended the local comprehensive school. No reply. He rang the bell continuously until it stuck in the "on" position, then beat a hasty retreat around the back of the house. John pegged it on the way to the back door and he became Hymie again. That didn't help much, but at least he knew who he was. He tried the door handle nervously and was surprised to find it open; not generally a good sign.

Adopting the bluff manner of an invited but clueless guest, he breezed through what appeared to be the kitchen and made his way into the lounge.

Trivial Pursuit lay facedown on the shag pile, a TV dinner slid tortuously down the far wall and a man's decapitated body sat bolt upright in the comfy chair, blood still oozing from the severed neck.

The wallpaper was liberally spattered with blood and the stench of death hung in the air. Hymie surveyed the room in stunned silence until his gaze was arrested by another horrific spectacle, the sight of the dead man's head, sitting grotesquely in a plant pot on the mantelpiece, its features frozen in a macabre grimace. It was the final straw.

"Blllaaaaaaaaa...yeeuuuuuurrrk!"

He vomited last night's pizza everywhere. He had been a detective for eight years without once seeing a dead body. He'd heard about such things of course. He'd even seen the odd dead pet; Mrs Timmins' cat Tiddles, which had jumped out of a beech tree and broken its neck as he was shinning along the branch to retrieve it. Yet nothing had prepared him for *this*.

It was only then he became aware that he had company.

"Banzaiiiiiiieeeee!!"

Hymie turned to find himself staring into the wild-eyed face of his would-be executioner, a diminutive oriental dressed entirely in black, the finely honed blade of his ancient samurai sword poised to create two H Goldmans where before there had been but one.

"Flip!" he thought, with panic-stricken understatement, and then he fell to the floor and grovelled pitifully.

"I've seen nothing; I'll say nothing...to no one, never. Look, I have money...take it; take my car, my life insurance...anything you like. I only came to read the meter," he gibbered, method acting as John the gasman to the last.

His assailant appeared unmoved. Lifting the sword until it was stretched at arm's length above his head he began its murderous descent on the southernmost slopes of Goldman's neck.

Hymie closed his eyes and began to think of his schooldays.

"Boy, what a shit life!"

BLAM! BLAM! BLAM!

Three gunshots rang out and the room was bathed in cordite fumes. Hymie opened his eyes. The smoke cleared to reveal his attacker, prostrate on the floor and wearing three rather large holes. Most of his anatomy was now vacationing in different parts of the room.

Standing behind the corpse and racking the slide of an outsized handgun stood the remarkable Miss Turner.

"J, J, J, Janis!"

"Hello, Mr Goldman, I thought you might need some help."

"But how, why, when? What I mean to say is…I thought…?"

"You thought that after those guys had taken the last of the office furniture you'd never see me again. You told me to take the day off, because you couldn't face telling me I was out of a job, but you're wrong, you know – it's not over yet."

"How did you know where to find me?"

"After I thought it through, I went into the office just in time to see you driving off in your car, so I followed you. Easy."

"And the gun?"

"Oh, I always carry that. Well, you have to when you live in Finsbury Park."

From the corner of his eye he caught sight of a glittering golden figurine on the mantelpiece. He pocketed it hastily. It might be a pig and it might not. Either way, it would pay for some new office furniture.

"Let's get the hell out of here," he said.

"There may be more of them; we'll have to be careful how we get out."

"That's not what I wanted to hear, Janis." He was starting to hyperventilate.

"Where did you park your car?" she asked.

"Just around the corner, on Coleridge Way."

"Right, you climb through the window and I'll provide covering fire," said Janis.

He looked at her as though she had gone mad.

"I don't *do* windows, Jan," said Hymie emphatically. "Not since I was nearly killed, leaning out of one as a kid."

"There's no time to waste, Hymie. We all have to face our demons some time. I'll make sure we're not being followed, then meet you at your car in five minutes."

He looked at her dubiously, then at the gun in her hand and finally at the vomit-strewn carpet.

"We don't want to be here when the owner gets home," he said, reflectively.

He pushed open the window, climbed out onto the crazy paving and ran as though his life depended on it for his car. Gunshots rang out in the cottage. Once back in the driver's seat he closed his eyes and put his head in his hands. He hoped Janis was okay, because he was about as much use to her as a chocolate teapot. The next five minutes seemed to last for hours, but then Janis arrived, climbed in beside him and he drove off as quickly and unobtrusively as it was possible to do, in a car that sounded like the mating call of an African bull elephant.

"What happened?" he asked.

"There were two more of them upstairs," said Janis.

"And you *killed* them?" He couldn't quite believe any of this was happening, but he had lost his tenuous grip on reality and didn't doubt the facts for a minute.

"It was purely self-defence," she said.

He drove in no particular direction, for miles, ending up at a motorway service station, where they sat in the cafeteria, talking in hushed tones.

To the casual observer he looked just like any other deadbeat: pale complexion, staring eyes, and with the indefinable aroma of regurgitated pizza. To the trained eye, however, Hymie Goldman was a man in shock, a man who had come too close for comfort to the grim reaper.

He sat motionless in the hard plastic chair, staring into the cold black depths of his neglected coffee. It seemed to mirror the bottomless void within him.

Janis by contrast was perfectly relaxed, or as relaxed as one can be in a motorway service area. She leant back, drawing steadily on her Havana cigar, and released perfectly formed smoke rings above her erstwhile employer's bowed head.

"Come on, pull yourself together. You must have seen a corpse before now," she said.

"Never. Look, Jan, I'm just not *that* sort of detective. If I've given you that impression then I'm sorry. I'm allergic to guns, bullets, knives, swords and anything else whose sole purpose is to kill. I've got to take this to the police. Will you come with me?"

"Are you crazy? After your last court appearance they're just looking for an excuse to pull you in. Given half a chance they'd lock you up and throw away the key! Your only option is to see the case through to the end. *Then* go and see the police if you must, but only when you know and can prove all the facts."

She was so cool, so level-headed, so worldly to be someone's assistant, let alone his.

"I could be dead by then!" Hymie protested.

"So? End of story. Do you want to be a missing-pet investigator all your life? Live a little!"

He didn't look exactly convinced.

"I have a phone call to make," he resolved finally.

"The police?" she queried.

"My client."

"Now you're thinking straight. Better still, let's go and see her together," volunteered Janis.

"What makes you think it's a woman, Jan, when this is a new case and you've never met the client?"

He was sharper than he looked, but Janis retained her composure.

"Just call it feminine intuition. You could certainly use some."

They made an unlikely pair heading for the service station car park; the short, overweight scruff-bag and the elegant young woman smoking a cigar. They could have passed for a circus novelty act, but not much else.

Hymie revved up the Zebaguchi's six-cylinder engine until all eyes around them were fixed on the source of the apocalyptic noise. Having no social awareness and little environmental conscience, Goldman remained in a pitiful state of ignorance about the state of the ozone layer and thought that CFC was a football team.

Since by now he had lost his client's business card, Hymie was forced to drive around the district aimlessly, in the hope of recognising some familiar landmark that would lead him to Lucy Scarlatti. On the whole he would have made a better vacuum-cleaner salesman than he did a private investigator.

Perhaps he should be looking out for a trail of dazed-looking males, he reflected.

Some hours later he finally spotted the telltale black Porsche and pulled over. Taking Janis with him for protection, he rang the bell.

A Big Ben door chime? He didn't remember it but the last time he'd been there his mind had been elsewhere. Besides, why would his client ring her own bell?

There was no reply, so he rang again, wincing as the chime resumed its assault on good taste. The door opened very slightly, held close on a security chain.

"Who is it?" asked Lucy Scarlatti.

"The man from Del Monte, who do you flamin' think!"

Hymie's nerves were beginning to unravel.

"Goldman! About time, where the hell have you been?"

"To a funeral, lady, and it was nearly mine. Now let me in, I need some answers!"

Lucy Scarlatti led him into the lounge of her tastelessly furnished apartment. Outside, Janis loaded six rounds of ammunition into the chambers of her pistol, slipped the gun into her handbag and walked casually into the flat.

Meanwhile, Hymie sprawled across an enormous scarlet satin beanbag, while Lucy Scarlatti mixed two extra-dry

Martinis at her cocktail bar, blithely unaware of the approaching peril now lurking in her reception hall.

"Did you bring the statuette?" she asked.

"Sure, but things weren't exactly straightforward," he replied.

She handed him a Martini, waiting to hear the additional cost of the complications.

He took it carefully, but his hand was shaking so much that most of it was spilt down his trousers before it ever reached his mouth.

"I'd be pushing up daisies if it wasn't for…"

She'd stopped listening to him and stood with her eyes transfixed on the shadowy figure emerging through the doorway.

Framed against the skylight behind Hymie stood Janis, her automatic trained on Lucy Scarlatti and with a ruthless glint in her cold blue eyes.

"Steffanie!"

It was Lucy Scarlatti's last word.

Part Five

A sadder but no wiser man, Hymie rose the morrow morn. His eyes flickered open. He was alive. Boy, did his head hurt, and he couldn't see properly out of his left eye. Then he suddenly became aware of the hospital ward around him and started desperately trying to recall his recent past.

Something was seriously wrong. Someone was dead. His client! He'd lost his client! Yet nothing quite seemed to fall into place, there was only the terrible pain in his head and eyes and odd snatches of a dreadful series of events.

"Nurse! Help me!" he cried.

"Calm down, Mr Goldman, you've lost a lot of blood."

"How do you know my name?" he snapped, paranoia flooding into his brain.

"It says it on your chart."

"Of course. How long have I been here?"

"Two days. Now you really must rest, Mr Goldman."

"Two days!! But anything could have happened in two days!"

"If you don't calm down I'll have to sedate you," said the nurse.

Hymie closed his eyes. Slowly the memories began to return.

That ridiculous schoolgirl Janis, the one I thought looked twenty-five…she *was* twenty-five! What a bitch! She must have shot my client and left me for dead. Whoa, hang on, it all sounds totally absurd…why would she? No one would ever believe it, even if it were true.

A man in a white coat approached the end of his bed, picked up his chart and frowned at the graph.

"Will I live, Doctor?" asked Hymie.

"According to this chart, you're already dead, Mr…"

"Goldman," added Hymie, hesitantly. It took a while to adjust to being dead.

"But there's very probably a perfectly logical explanation," he said, trying to be reassuring.

"Sorry, Doctor, they forgot to remove his chart after the last patient checked out," remarked the nurse, sheepishly.

"Checked out? You mean the poor soul died in this bed?!" exclaimed Hymie, shocked.

"Inevitably, with the best will in the world, patients do die, Mr Goldman, and we can't throw them out of their beds *before* it happens, to spare the feelings of those who replace them, now can we?" said the doctor, forgetting his basic bedside manner in his irritation.

"Sorry, you're right, of course. Can you tell me what happened to *me*, Doctor? I don't seem to be able to remember the last two days."

"Ah, amnesia, it's often a factor in cases of this sort," remarked the doctor, staring absently into space.

"Cases of what sort?" asked Hymie.

"Eh?"

"You mentioned amnesia, Doctor."

"Well, is it any wonder, man? Working around the clock without proper support, I've been twenty hours on the ward without a toilet break, I'm bursting for a…"

"Tea, Mr Goldman?" asked the nurse.

"Yes please, nurse."

"You're a lucky man, Mr Goldberg," resumed the eccentric medic. You seem to have received a glancing blow from a bullet. Half an inch lower and you wouldn't be here now. I'm afraid it's doubtful whether you'll ever see properly out of your left eye again, but otherwise you should make a full recovery with plenty of rest." He smiled at Hymie, stifling a yawn.

"Thank you, Doctor, but I'm working to a deadline."

"You will be, Mr Goldstein, if you don't get some sleep right now. I understand the police will want to interview you in the morning, so get some rest, man."

Hymie closed his eyes and listened until he heard the doctor's footsteps shuffling down the corridor. Gradually the ward became quiet as the light outside faded first into dusk and then into the sable mantle of night's darkest bower. In his mind's eye he could see nothing but corpses, mutilated rotten cadavers, stretching out in all directions. Ugh! A shiver ran down his spine. The only people Hymie had ever known go into hospital had left it in a box.

He surveyed the ward around him. The next bed seemed to be ring-fenced with curtains. He couldn't be sure who, or indeed if anyone, was in there, though there was a sign at the foot of the bed which said simply, "MRS A". Whoever she was, she was a deep sleeper.

He tried to sit up, but every movement seemed to cause him pain. He felt like Mrs Timmins' cat must have done on first hitting the pavement, except that *he* was still very much alive. The desire for revenge would keep him so, of that he was sure.

Bandages covered most of his head and shoulders. He knew he must look like a refugee from *The Rocky Horror Show*, but perhaps the bandages could help conceal his identity. If only he could get out of the ward. His clothes were gone; all he had was the regulation-issue nightgown with the defective ties at the back and a draft around his nether regions.

Pushing the screens aside he walked down the central aisle. It was an experiment in mind over matter; if they didn't mind and he didn't matter, perhaps he could just walk straight out of there. Unfortunately, he had bargained without the ever-watchful Inspector Ray Decca and his dedicated sergeant, Barry Terse. They weren't about to lose the only witness they had to a murder, even if that witness was as unreliable as Hymie Goldman.

"Is that '*im*, guv? The nutter with the bandaged head?" asked Terse.

"Who else would it be, Sergeant? Queen Nefertiti?"

"Oi, you, Goldman! This is Finchley Memorial Hospital, not a fashion parade," added Terse, distractedly trying to recover his change from the coffee machine with a number-ten boot.

Hymie walked on unheeding. Perhaps if he could convince himself that they were just illusions, they would really disappear. Some chance.

"Hold it right there, Goldman," said Inspector Decca.

Part Six

On the following morning, Hymie sat up in his hospital bed and prepared to give his statement to the police. He didn't expect it to take long, as he couldn't remember much. It hadn't been a good day for him; he'd survived a trip to South Mimms, only to be shot in the Docklands. All very painful and humiliating.

"My name is Decca, Mr Goldman – D-E-C-C-A, but *Inspector* Decca to you. Before you ask, no, I don't own a record company and my first name isn't Desmond. Some of the lads call me Chief or Guv, rivals call me Big Ears on account of how I hear about things before they happen, and the criminal fraternity calls me Cluedo, because…"

"You always assume the crime was committed in the library with a candlestick?"

"I solve all my cases by a process of deductive reasoning. I shall put your last remark down to the blow to the head you received recently," concluded Decca.

He was about to remark that it would probably be the first of several Goldman would receive, if he didn't co-operate with the police enquiry, but thought better of it. Times were changing and he couldn't face the additional paperwork.

"Thank you, Inspector," said Hymie.

"Don't mention it. Now then, about a week ago I received a summons from my boss…"

"Speeding ticket?" Hymie, as ever, couldn't resist an easy quip.

"He handed me your file and told me to take matters in hand. I'd heard you were the sort of low-life scum that gives private investigators a bad name, and a quick perusal of your file did nothing to change my mind. It came as no surprise that you were wanted for eighty-six road traffic violations."

"Thirty-five!"

"That's just *this* year's. A joker like you shouldn't be left in charge of a bicycle, let alone anything with a turbo-charged engine, but this was a matter my sergeant could have sorted in his sleep. As you can probably guess, I'm here about a far more serious matter; about a murder, in fact, and you are my chief suspect."

"Murder? Me? Look at me. Thirty-eight, short, fat and balding, covered in bandages and lucky to be alive. Hardly a dangerous killer, am I? You're barking…"

"Watch it, Goldman!"

"…up the wrong tree, Inspector."

"You really are as stupid as you look, aren't you, Goldman! We were there when the ambulance took you away. We know all about the girl. We have you at the scene of the crime; you had the opportunity and the motive. We even have the murder weapon with your prints on."

"Not a candlestick, I suppose?" asked Hymie, impulsively, in the absence of anything sensible to say.

"When you're in a hole, son, stop digging! Otherwise I don't fancy your chances of avoiding a long prison stretch!"

"Look, Inspector, you may know all these things, but frankly I don't. The murdered woman was my client."

"What was her name?" asked Decca.

"Lucy Scarlatti. She hired me to recover a family heirloom from her sister. I was getting nowhere; I couldn't even find her sister," he lied.

"So you killed her, Goldman?"

"Why *would* I, Inspector? You'd have to be stark raving mad to believe that."

"You found the heirloom, went to her flat, and offered to sell it to her for more money than she was willing or able to pay. She refused and you shot her dead."

"I repeat, Inspector, why? More to the point, there must have been someone else present to account for *my* injuries. Whoever shot me must have killed my client and stolen her property."

"So, who *was* with you, Goldman?"

"No one," he lied, inexplicably; even to himself. "I went to see Lucy Scarlatti alone, to tell her the case was proving too difficult for me and that I would reluctantly have to repay a part of the retainer. The next thing I remember is waking up here, with a terrible pain in my head, and being told that I'd been shot and my client killed. Now you're trying to fit me up for a murder I didn't commit. It's been the worst day of my life."

"All very sad, I'm sure, but it doesn't alter the fact that your former client is dead and you were the last person to see her alive. Okay, Goldman, let's play devil's advocate. If it wasn't you, then who?" The Inspector looked triumphant, as though he had a tricky suspect on the ropes.

"Her sister, Steffanie," replied Hymie, coolly. "It stands to reason. According to my client they hated each other and her sister had stolen this heirloom from her. Perhaps it was easier to kill her than to give it back."

"What was this heirloom, Goldman?"

"A golden statuette of a pig."

"You're having a laugh. A golden *pig*? If I find you've been pulling my plonker you may find yourself in here for longer than expected! Are you sure it wasn't a platinum cow or a diamond-encrusted sheep?"

"Now you're just being ridiculous," said Hymie, testily.

"Believe me, *you're* the one looking ridiculous," snapped Decca. "Have you seen yourself in the mirror lately? Anyhow, when did you last see your client alive?"

"Two nights ago, at her flat."

"You mean 35 Riverside Drive?"

"If you say so, Inspector, I've lost my address book."

"You said you were alone together?"

"How can you be alone *together*?" Hymie mocked, unwisely.

"Alone with the client! Don't try to be funny, Goldman. This is a *murder* investigation. Even these days, that means several years in prison with some real low-life scum. Then when you get out you'll find your licence as an investigator has been revoked."

"I know, you're right, Inspector, I'm not feeling myself at the moment."

"I can see that. Tell me, where did you get the gun?"

"I swear to God, I've never carried a gun. It's not my scene. People who play with matches get burned," added Hymie, obscurely.

"Where did it come from then? Your client?" Decca was like a dog with a bone.

"I don't carry a gun, I don't own one, and I didn't shoot Lucy Scarlatti," repeated Hymie, emphatically.

"But you know who did…"

"Like I told you, Inspector, it must have been her sister."

"You saw her at the flat?"

"Yes…no, well, someone came up behind me. One minute I was talking to Lucy Scarlatti, trying to get out of the assignment, then there was a gunshot behind me. She fell down and I remember trying to turn around to see who it was…and that's all I remember."

"And you expect me to believe this, Goldman?"

"Yes, because it's the truth," he replied, simply.

Decca looked at his watch. "Okay, let's leave it there for now. Sergeant Terse will be posted outside the ward until you're able to leave, and then I'd like you to come down to the station for a proper interview. I suggest you get your story straight by then. One last question, what were you *really* trying to recover for Lucy Scarlatti?"

Hymie paused. "Her father's diary," he said. "It had some clue in it about where he buried a treasure." He sensed that the inspector needed some other line of enquiry to pursue; to avoid jumping to conclusions about *his* guilt, but force of habit made him lie. Knowledge was power, even if you hardly had any.

Decca stared intently at Goldman for a moment, weighing him up.

"Thank you," he said, and left.

Part Seven

Hymie lay in his hospital bed, planning his escape. He wasn't exactly Harry Houdini, but then this wasn't quite maximum security. Surely he could get past that dozy police sergeant waiting outside the ward? He just needed a plausible disguise. Had Hymie but known it, Sergeant Terse was busy trying to chat up the nurse on night duty down the corridor and, for once, not making his usual hash of it.

"Can I have a look at your truncheon, Sergeant?" asked the nurse.

"Any time, love," replied Terse, grinning inanely.

"Ooh, isn't it *hard*."

"Yeah, like the rest of me. If it could talk it could tell you a few stories and no mistake," he said, with a winning smile.

In the ward all was dark and quiet; still as the grave. Well, apart from a few hacking coughs and the persistent bleeping of a clapped-out NHS heart monitor.

Hymie closed his eyes and drifted back into sleep. Sleeping was something he excelled at, though it was hardly a bankable skill. His eyelids flickered involuntarily as he began to dream. Fluffy white sheep were trampolining all over the bouncy castle of his brain. Somewhere in its deepest recesses he could hear a voice he recognised.

"Wake up, you lazy twit! There you go again, sleeping on the job."

"Wassermarrer?" spluttered Hymie.

"Look, son, don't lie there like a great green vegetable, cases don't solve *themselves*, you know!"

"What is this, a repeat of Randall and flipping Hopkirk? If so, you must be the dead one…Hopkirk."

"Less of your lip. Wake up this instant, do you hear?"

So he did, or tried to. He opened his eyes, sat up and looked around. A short grizzled little man with white hair and side whiskers was standing at the foot of his bed.

"*Dad*?! What are *you* doing here? Don't you realise you've been dead for the last five years?"

"Oh, *dead*, is it! I've got more life in me than you, you quitter! I may be dead, you young upstart, but at least I'm not farting about waiting for someone to dump on me from a great height, like you. You're a disgrace to the name of Shaw."

"Ah, yes, well…I was going to tell you about that."

"About what?" asked his ghostly father, suspiciously.

"Oh, it'll keep. Look, Dad, it's very kind of you to drop by like this, but…"

Suddenly the absurdity of the situation hit Hymie like a brick between the eyes. He was arguing with a mirage…or a ghost…or a dream…or *something that shouldn't be there.*

"Dad nothing! I didn't say anything when you threw in your apprenticeship as an electrician, I tried to teach you the tricks of the investigations business…and failed, and I'd planned to sell the business and leave you with a nestegg…"

"Only you died first. You never kept an opinion to yourself when you were alive and now it seems you can't stop yourself even after death…and *I'm* supposed to be the one with the problem."

"Less of it, you layabout, hear me out! You were never

suited to the business, it's true, but I finally realised that you'd earned the right to make your own mistakes. Now I'm sure as hell not going to stand idly by and watch you throw the family business down the pan. Get out of bed and solve this case, like I taught you. Show me what you can do!" So saying, the grumpy apparition dematerialised through the wall.

After the initial shock had passed, Hymie was gracious enough to concede that the old illusion may just have had a point. Gathering his nightgown about him with a flourish, he pulled the bandages down over his nose and mouth at a raffish angle, suggesting the merest impression of a surgeon's mask, and raced down the corridor. Thus it was that the scantily clad detective returned to his case.

He tiptoed cautiously past the somnolent copper on watch, PC Reidy, Terse's relief, a former civil servant who had been dismissed for showing excessive initiative. Then, pulling open the latticed doors of the first service lift he came to, Hymie stepped inside.

WHOOSH!

A sudden rush of blood to the head. A sensation of cold air whistling through what was left of his hair and the laundry chute loomed up at him as he plummeted to certain death.

WHUMPH!

Certain death never sounded like that. It usually involved the crunch of mangled bones or the splattering of one's soft tissues. Not for Hymie; he came to rest in a pile of dirty laundry with nothing worse than mild concussion. Not nice of course; dirty underpants in the face, but a million miles from being stone dead.

"Yrrgh! Arrgh!" he groaned, eloquent to a fault.

"You can't kip in 'ere, mate. Try the park down the road. Who the 'ell are you anyway?" enquired a passing porter.

Stumbling clumsily through the emergency exit, he fell down a short flight of stairs, banged his head on the wall for luck and burst through the fire door, tripping the alarm as a grand finale. As the door flapped wildly in the breeze, the sound of bells filled the air. All he knew was that he had to get as far away as possible as quickly as he could. Even by his own sartorial standards, he looked a real mess and he felt worse than he would have thought possible.

Hymie instinctively found himself heading for the park. He needed time and space to assess where the last few nightmarish days had left him. Half naked, bandaged and bloody, he kept to the shadows for fear of arrest or identification as a Young Conservative on his way home from a fancy dress party. He scowled at passers-by and they gave him a wide berth.

The facts were certainly grim; he was wanted for a murder he hadn't committed by a criminal justice system that didn't much care if it got the right man or not. Of course, he'd probably only get a suspended sentence for the murder, it was the parking offences that *really* worried him.

North Finchley's first private detective to be listed in *Catering World* shivered in the park for ten minutes before deciding that hypothermia wasn't a good career move and what he really needed was pizza, preferably from Benny Baker's. Benny was the next best thing to a really good friend, a really old creditor.

For once the lack of bus fare didn't seem to matter. The driver assumed he was an escaped mental patient and public spiritedly let him on for nothing. He left the bus at Finchley Central bus depot and headed straight for Benny's. The Unbeatable Bakery was looking sorrier for itself than usual; a bulb had fused in the neon sign outside, rendering the pizzas "Un*eatable*". The shop had long since closed for the day, but Hymie rang the bell and a light came on in the upstairs flat. A window opened and Benny poked his head out cautiously.

"Who the heck's calling in the middle of the night? Don't you loonies got homes to go to?"

"Benny, it's me, Hymie Goldman. I've got the money I owe you."

"Goldman? Is that really you? You look like some old tramp. Come to think of it, you are..."

"Benny, I need help..."

"I never doubted it. Come here, stand under the light." Hymie obliged by walking into the streetlamp.

"Jeez, Goldman, you're in a right state, mate. What's with the bandages? You haven't joined the Young Conservatives, surely?"

"Benny, I hate to ask, but it's urgent. You couldn't rustle up some old clothes and a pizza, could you?"

"I'd heard you were wanted by the police, H, but I never figured they would cut up so rough over forty-eight parking offences. You look ruddy awful."

"Awful's right. As for the fines, it's only thirty-five, but I'm in serious need of a few hours' kip, if you've got a spare sofa, Ben."

"Well, just this once, H. I'll come down and let you in."

"You're the best, Benny."

Moments later he appeared at the door, led Hymie through the restaurant and up the backstairs into his flat. From the look of his furnishings, Benny's business was clearly booming. The pizza king of North London draped a couple of black garbage sacks across his sofa and bade his old acquaintance sit down. Over a glass or three of Chardonnay they reminisced about days and mutual friends long since gone.

"What are you calling yourself these days, H?" asked Benny.

"Oh, it's still Hymie, Ben. Well, it got rather confusing after a while; I'd pick up a phone and not know which name to answer to."

"I never understood what was wrong with Artie. Still, you don't change much otherwise. So, you're hungry, eh?"

"Starving. I could eat my way through the menu twice, Ben."

"Not on the house, H, but I can certainly rustle you up a pizza. How about I give you a cookery lesson? Well, I'm never gonna get rich selling you pizzas, the state your finances are in, so I may as well help you avoid dying of starvation. I'm going to teach you a life skill you won't learn anywhere else, H; how to make the best pizza in the world."

Hymie began to salivate, like a Pavlovian dog on hearing the dinner gong.

Benny donned his white chef's hat and was instantly transformed into the culinary wizard he had always been. Presentation was everything.

"Will it take long, Benny? Only my stomach thinks my throat's been cut."

"You can't rush perfection, H."

"Don't you have anything *average* you could serve up in a couple of minutes?"

Dismissing the remark as unworthy with a curt shake of the head, Benny resumed the impromptu demonstration of his peerless cooking skills.

Minutes later, Hymie was tucking into the best pizza he had ever tasted.

"Benny, you reign supreme. Abso-ruddy-lutely supreme, mate."

Benny smiled and left his guest to his thoughts.

"I'll put some clothes outside the door for when you get up, H. Make sure you're out by nine a.m., I don't want you upsetting the staff with your appearance."

"Will do, Ben, and thanks."

He was back on track now, thought Hymie; he only had to beat the murder rap, solve the case of the golden pig and sell the business to Ceefer Capital and it would all be hunky-dory. Easy.

Part Eight

Back in his office at the police station, Inspector Ray Decca was dozing at his desk. He had spent a long hard night piecing together the few strands of evidence available. It didn't amount to a hill of baked beans. He was a frustrated perfectionist and hated having loose ends in his investigation. The biggest loose end of all seemed to be Hymie Goldman.

Three corpses in two days: one man decapitated in some ritualistic gangland execution and two ventilated at close range by what looked like the same gun. Someone had seen a short fat guy walking away from the scene of crime one, and although not a betting man, he would have put his gold cufflinks on it being Goldman. Still, however much he tried to imagine it, he couldn't see Goldman killing anyone, with or without a gun. Boring them to death or offending them with his appalling dress sense, perhaps.

Terse and Reidy had cocked up big time and their number one suspect was on the loose, but he didn't seriously believe that Goldman constituted a real threat to society, probably less of one than Terse, anyway.

Decca began to snore. His chair, which had been tilted back against the office wall, started to slide down it. Just as he began to overbalance there was a knock on the door that sounded like an air raid on Iraq. Sergeant Terse entered.

Decca sprang up in his chair and knocked the contents of his half-empty coffee cup all over the files on his desk.

"Terse, you're a flaming idiot!"

"Yes, Chief."

"What do you want?"

"You asked me to let you know if I discovered any leads, sir."

"The mind boggles, Terse...tell me all."

"We've had a positive ID on the dead Chink, sir. A guy named Chiu Mann. Nasty piece of work, Chief: a hit man for the Triads."

"You don't say, Terse, I never would have guessed it."

Sarcasm was wasted on him.

"Thank you, sir," said Terse, beaming. Perhaps there was hope for him yet.

"Just leave me the file. Oh, and Terse..."

"Sir?"

"Make sure you're on surveillance duty at Goldman's office bright and early, eh? We don't want a repeat performance of the hospital fiasco, do we?!"

"No, sir."

So saying, the pride of Finchley nick sloped off to arrange the mother of all surveillances. He'd show that smart ass inspector and that toe rag Goldman. No one messed with Barry Terse.

Decca reviewed the files once more. His instinct told him that three corpses in two days must be connected. But how?

Body number one turned out to belong to a guy called Tony Martino, a small-time drug-pusher with rumoured links to the Triads' cartel. It was fairly safe to assume he'd fallen foul of his Chinese paymasters and been topped by the professional hit man, Chiu Mann.

Body number two had been the hit man himself. Mann had been a ruthless killer, Red Pole for the Second Lodge, so whoever had shot him must have taken him by surprise. The *gun* was mightier than the sword, not the pen. Just imagine trying to fend off a mad samurai warrior with a Biro! No chance.

Body number three was the mystery woman, Lucy Scarlatti, young, beautiful, and seemingly affluent, yet she had been tragically misinformed. She had hired Goldman as a private investigator, though if you believed him it was only to recover a diary from her sister. The Girl Guides could have handled that...and yet Goldman claimed he was about to drop the case as being too difficult for him. Who did he think he was kidding?

If Goldman had been there when Martino died, and was still walking around, which he clearly was, then either Goldman must be the greatest actor this side of Stratford, a level-headed killing machine masquerading as a total idiot; or he was a lucky blighter and the real killer was still walking the streets.

On balance he favoured the latter theory, which meant that whether he knew it or not, Goldman was their only direct link with the real killer. There was still no motive for the second and third murders. Was it really all about drugs? If so, he'd have to turn it over to the Drug Squad and he'd miss the best chance of promotion he'd had in ages. Nah, it couldn't be just about drugs, when you came to think of it. Goldman had said something about a diary and even if you didn't really take anything he said as kosher it was a good pretext for extending the investigation.

One thing was for sure: Goldman was mixing in lethal company, and if they didn't pull him in sooner rather than later he'd be found floating in the Thames or propping up some motorway bridge. That was why Terse and the lads would be staking out his office and locating all his known associates. Decca groaned at the thought of all the overtime he would have to sign off, and what his commanding officer would have to say at the next budget review meeting. Ruddy bean counters!

Part Nine

Benny had unearthed some groovy clothes for Hymie from the back of his wardrobe – collectors' items that probably hadn't seen the light of day since 1969. Hymie, who couldn't afford to be choosy, and had never understood fashion, put them on gratefully.

The ensemble was nothing if not bold – a bright orange pullover, some bell-bottomed trousers in turquoise, an old pair of trainers and a flat cap of the tweedy variety, all topped off with a promotional padded jacket, bearing the slogan "You can't beat Benny's" in gold transfer lettering across the back. A pair of sunglasses helped conceal his injured eye.

"What are your plans, H?"

"Oh, you know...keeping a low profile."

"You'll be fine," Benny reassured him.

"Yeah, as long as I don't go out in daylight in these clothes," smirked Hymie.

"Will you be going to the police?"

"I don't think they can help me, Ben. They'd probably bang me up for every open case on their books. I know that sounds paranoid...but everyone really is out to get me," confided Hymie.

"How's the case going?" Benny asked.

"Technically I don't have a case. My client's dead so I won't get paid and yet I can't find it in me just to walk away. There's such a thing as professional pride, you know."

"Well, I never thought I'd live to hear you say that, H, you old fraud."

"This is my greatest case, Ben. I'm on the trail of a valuable *objêt*."

"How much is it worth?"

"Ooh...fifty, maybe a hundred."

"What, quid?"

"No, grand, you Charlie."

"That's a lot of mozzarella, H."

"No, seriously, Ben, the stakes are high."

"The only catch is, Hymie, people get killed for that kind of money."

"It had crossed my mind too. I'm just not cut out for dodging bullets. Finding lost cats on a good day, yes; getting shot at, no. Look at me; nerves cut to ribbons, bandages all over my head and I haven't got the faintest idea who's behind it all or what's going to happen next."

"Like you said, you should keep a low profile, H. Maybe even go abroad."

"My profile can't get any lower, Ben. Trouble is, the only people who know I exist have got it in for me and I can't even afford the tube fare to Golders Green, so emigration is a non-starter."

Benny failed to suppress a snigger. He would have been a real asset to the Samaritans.

"It's all very well you laughing, mate, I'm in it up to my neck and there's another delivery of shit expected any minute," said Hymie. "I should have stuck to investigating lost pets; at least they don't try to kill you!"

"I'm sorry to hear it, H, here's a few quid for tube fares anyway. Be lucky."

"Thanks, Benny, you've been great. I don't want you getting caught up in the crossfire, so I'm going. If anyone asks you about me, just tell them you haven't seen me in weeks. It's almost true. When I sort everything out I'll pay you back big time."

Benny stepped over to the window and peered through the chink in the blinds.

"Hold on a minute, H. It looks like someone's watching your office."

Hymie took a look for himself. Aftab Hamid was opening up his newsagent's, a few long-distance lorry drivers were filing into the Black Kat for the cardiac special fry-up, and three vehicles were parked at the kerb outside 792A Finchley Road.

"Now who could that be?" wondered Hymie, out loud.

"Well, *you're* the detective, but from what you've been telling me it's probably the police."

"That's just what I was thinking, Ben," said Hymie, looking embarrassed.

"Except for the white transit, of course," said Benny.

"Oh, why do you say that?"

"It belongs to my nephew, Ricky, and he's probably snogging his bird in the back. He constantly complains of having nowhere to go. Of course, the blue transit belongs to that roadie who's just started working for the opera singer," added Benny. "But if you ask me, they may be more than just good friends..."

"Really? So, what about the green Renault?" asked Hymie, intrigued.

"You figure it, H, I've just told you two out of three, for heaven's sake!"

"No sweat, Ben. Look, I'll just leave by the back door and slip down the side passage. Thanks again for all your help."

The side alley leading to Benny's rear entrance offered an excellent if restricted view of the pavement outside his own office, so Hymie spent a few minutes standing in the shadows observing proceedings. The green Renault had to be an unmarked police car. There was a hefty guy with a crew cut in the back who reminded him of that Neanderthal, Terse, and a driver who could have passed for a close relative.

Times must be tough in the Met, reflected Hymie as he examined the Renault 25 in more detail. The wings were pockmarked with corrosion spots and someone had sprayed

"Frog Shit!" in fluorescent pink along the driver's door. It was probably Terse's idea of a joke.

Suddenly the doors of the blue transit flew open. Ha! Benny had been wrong. Two uniformed policemen jumped out and walked back to the Renault. Terse seemed to be in charge. After a brief exchange the uniformed duo headed along the pavement towards the Black Kat.

Hymie frowned. If they were searching door-to-door they needed him and it was probably only a matter of time before they found him. Still, he wasn't going to hand himself in; as much as he feared being on the loose with a killer at large, at least he wasn't a sitting duck in a police cell. Breaking his cover, he headed down the road away from his office. He passed Aftab's shop. The dozy shopkeeper was engrossed in something on the counter and didn't notice him. Probably one of those Swedish imports.

There were two public phone boxes, back-to-back, on the pavement, just past the newsagent's. He paused, then entered one. Lifting the receiver he placed a washer in the coin slot and held an imaginary conversation with someone on the other end. It gave him the chance to keep his office under surveillance from a safer distance.

"I must be stark staring mad to leave a nice warm hospital bed for this," he thought. "What good am I doing here anyway? Watching a bunch of coppers trying to find me won't solve anything."

He was on the point of leaving when his gaze was arrested by the sight of Janis emerging from the small car park behind Hamid's. She clocked the unmarked police car and started walking away, directly towards Hymie. Behind the sunglasses he closed his good eye and raised his hands to his face in a despairing gesture.

"Why *me*, God?" he said aloud.

He had tried to work it out, he really had. He had given it his best shot, but the harder he tried, the more confusing it all became. This case was like his life; a huge shattered looking glass, whose splintered shards had become an increasingly distorted series of unrelated images. All his points of reference seemed to be in a state of flux and he could discern no pattern in the chaos. Janis, who had been his rock, might as well have turned to jelly; she now seemed to be batting for the other side. Had she really shot his client in cold blood and set him up for it? If so, was this whole ridiculous case simply about a golden pig? He could only presume Janis already had the flaming thing, because he certainly didn't.

With his good eye open he peeped between his fingers, half expecting the words "Game over" to flash in neon lights across the sky. The beautiful Miss Turner was opening the door to the other phone box and appeared not to have noticed him. She was now close enough to hear, but he was terrified of being recognised. Keeping his back turned towards her, he pulled up the new jacket's excuse for a collar and continued his own one-sided conversation in case she should begin to think he was listening to her.

He was at a loss to explain his fear of her. She was a killer, yes, and as such deserving of the greatest caution, but she had saved his life too. Had she spared him only to become the patsy for the murder of Lucy Scarlatti? He would have words with her at her next performance review. Ah, no, wrong again; those days were over.

Janis was deadly and unpredictable and she unsettled him, but he didn't know for certain that she had killed La Scarlatti. He hoped against hope that she was still on his side. For his part, he had lied to the police to protect her, yet he hadn't the faintest idea why he had done it. He wasn't about to find out the hard way.

He became increasingly curious to know what she was up to and tried to make some kind of sense out of the dribs and drabs of conversation he was able to overhear.

"You cowardly yellow turd...mumble, mumble."

"This is the last time...mumble, mumble."

"...so you say, mumble. Look, I want those numbers, mumble, mumble. Twenty-four, thirty-six, mumble, mumble. Tonight...right!"

She slammed down the receiver, scribbled something on

a piece of paper, and then retraced her steps back down the road.

Hymie's heartbeat took several minutes to return to its normal sloth and then he hastened to examine the vacated phone booth. Those numbers had sounded strangely familiar...his overdraft limit? No, he had it...it was that crazy Chinaman and his pairs of numbers! The call at the office must have been for Janis, but what were the numbers for?

He searched the booth but she had left no obvious clues; no box of matches bearing the name and address of the secret dope den, no map references, nothing. Yet she had written down some numbers.

He remembered one of the few things he had read, as an eager trainee, in *The Investigator's Handbook*, that you could recover a written message from a pencil rubbing of the book or blotter used to rest the writing paper on. He tried it and was delighted to learn that it worked.

The message simply read, "Rainbow Rooms 11 p.m., 24, 36, 42."

Tonight, she had clearly said *tonight*. This was one appointment with destiny he intended to keep. He didn't know yet what he would do when he arrived, but somehow he was going to be there.

Part Ten

Hymie stood on the southbound platform of a Northern Line station and watched the world go by. A young couple were kissing next to him and seemed to be in a world of their own, but although he existed in the same state he found it hard to remember the enthusiasms of youth. He had been married once, but it couldn't last.

"Duz deez wan go to Lundun, sur?"

He was about to tell the curious stranger in no uncertain terms that they *all* went to London, because it was a *big* place, but allowed himself to be seduced by the latter's use of the "s" word in relation to himself. He so rarely received even so slight or unintended a courtesy.

"No, mate, this one's for postal deliveries only. Try the other platform," he said, pointing across the station.

Soon his tube arrived, the doors hissed open and he was swallowed up into its monstrous mechanical belly. The only vacant seat was the one next to the wild-eyed Glaswegian drunk who smelt of urine. Recognising a fellow piece of flotsam washed up on life's shore, Hymie sat beside him.

The drunk goggled at him.

"Aaahm no sitten nexteryu, pal," he growled, and slouched off to be offensive elsewhere.

SHHTOOOM! The train disappeared into the shadowy world of subterranean tunnels in pursuit of timetable compliance while Hymie worked out his strategy for getting into the nightclub. Looking as he did, the options were strictly limited; the eccentric millionaire or the escaped mental patient in search of tea and sympathy.

Above ground, the tall, statuesque brunette with the opalescent eyes approached the double doors of the Rainbow Rooms' club and casino with a winning smile on her beautiful face. No one had ever refused her entry to a nightclub and they weren't about to start now. Although dressed like a million dollars, tonight she was slumming it, but she hadn't come to dance. Her name was Janis Turner and she had her own reasons for heading for the roulette table at eleven p.m.; to keep an assignation with her own unadulterated greed.

"Is Tony in tonight?" she asked the doorman.

"Tony who?" he queried.

"Lee."

"Oh, the croupier...I think he'll be in later."

She smiled at him. If he had been wearing glasses they would have steamed up.

"Is this the way to the Dragon Bar?" she asked.

"Over there, lady," he said, pointing.

Back on the Underground, the short podgy guy in the flat cap and charity-shop gear was catching up on his beauty sleep. Five or ten years would have been in order with a face like his. The serpentine sound of doors opening roused him just in time to disembark at London Bridge. Outside the station he hailed a taxi. The first driver put his foot down on spotting his potential fare and sped past the disreputable-looking PI in search of American tourists. The second pulled up for long enough to catch his destination and then decided to take the chance. Perhaps he'd pick up a fare back from the club.

It had been many years since Hymie had ventured into what could properly be described as a nightclub. With his planned big entrance as an incognito oil billionaire, the possibility that he might get turned away at the door, in the garish clobber Benny had provided, simply hadn't occurred to him. Apparently it *had* occurred to the doorman, a man mountain in a ridiculously small tuxedo.

"Can I help you, mate?"

"Waahl, hah there, buddy. Ahhm a-visiting yor liddle ol' country from Hoostun, Texas, an' ah thought ah'd lahk ter see wan o' yore casino boars."

"Sorry, members only, mate."

Close up, Hymie began to appreciate just how vast and imposing the bouncer actually was. He seemed to blot out the light completely. His chances of getting into the Rainbow Rooms were beginning to resemble the prospects of a one-legged man in an arse-kicking contest.

"Aahl mek it wuth yor wahl, buddy," he persisted.

He reluctantly proffered a dog-eared five-pound note.

The bouncer looked down disdainfully at the meagre bribe.

"Push off, Hank!"

Clearly the exaggerated American accent hadn't stacked up with Hymie's apparent deficiency of moolah and he had been dismissed as a fake, an impecunious phoney. The denizens of Texas hadn't hitherto been noted for their reluctance to part with their greenbacks on a big night out. Deflated, Hymie turned and began to walk back down the street. He stopped abruptly.

Something about the way the bouncer held himself and

the matching pair of cauliflower ears rang a distant bell. He turned back to examine the massive roadblock more closely.

"Hadn't you used to be Mad Mike Murphy?" asked Hymie, from a safe distance.

"What's it to you, mate? Coming here with your dodgy yank accent and your cheap bribes. I ought to smash your face in."

"I used to be Artie Shaw."

Blank look. Dawning recognition. Sunrise over the industrial park of his face.

"Artie Shaw! I remember. Are you still the same loser you always used to be?"

"Well, of course, I never aspired to the heights of being a professional chucker-out like yourself, but I do have my own business."

"No kiddin'?"

"Yes, it's the old family business…private investigations."

"So you're under cover then?" asked Mike.

"No, but I will be if you let me into the club."

"Look, I'm off duty in ten minutes, so if you can keep a low profile in the Dragon Lounge for that long, we can get a beer for old times' sake around the corner, if you like."

"Sounds like a plan. Which way is it?" asked Hymie.

"Just follow the lights and the din," said Mike.

Hymie passed through the double doors and followed the noise. It made a change from following his nose. Standing at the bar, dressed to kill, was the remarkable Miss Turner, a vision in Versace, Cuban heels and a cigar to match. Fidel would have been proud. Hymie couldn't tell if she was surprised to see him or not, she hid it so well.

"It's good to see you on your feet again, Mr Goldman. Look, er, Hymie, I've been trying to get in touch with you. The hospital didn't know where you'd gone so I thought I'd have to deal with it myself. You had a call from the Total Disaster Insurance Corporation. Apparently they were interested in retaining your services in trying to recover a golden statuette…"

"Of a pig?"

"Exactly."

Dare he believe her? Did this mean that she *didn't* know where the pig was and that she thought *he* might? Was there a "y" in the month?

"So it was insured? I wonder who by?" he speculated idly.

"Presumably by the owner, of course," said Janis.

"Yes, but who *owned* it? Perhaps no one *can* own a golden pig."

"You seem a little confused, Hymie. You should get more sleep."

"I will. Listen, Jan, you never did tell me what happened on the night Lucy Scarlatti died. You were there too, remember?"

"I feel terrible about it, Hymie, I really do. I just popped down the road to the off licence for some cigars and when I came back it was all over. The door was open and everything was in complete chaos. I phoned for an ambulance and the police and then drove home in your car. There wasn't really anything I could do by then and I didn't want to get involved with the police."

He nodded dumbly at her, not believing a word. He had seen her gun down a hired killer and, albeit that in doing so she had saved his life, such things leave an indelible impression.

She seemed to be getting edgy all of a sudden and he noticed it was almost eleven p.m. by the clock behind the bar.

"I have to go. They're sending a claims investigator to see you tomorrow."

"What time?"

"Eleven a.m. sharp."

"Is it safe to go back to the office then?"

"I said you'd meet them at Benny's."

"Are the police still crawling all over my office?" queried Hymie.

"No, they left today. They told me to let them know if you came back."

"Thanks, Jan."

"Don't mention it."

She turned and walked over to the casino.

"No sign of Tony Lee tonight, Mike?"

"He hasn't been in at all, Steffie. Maybe he's doing a double shift at the takeaway."

"Goodnight, Murphy."

"See you, gorgeous."

Hymie had followed at a discreet distance and overheard all that was said.

Why would Murphy be calling Janis Turner "Steffie" if it wasn't her name? Which of them had she duped, or was it both? And why did her name sound so familiar? He'd come to the club to find out what Janis Turner was up to and what the significance of the numbers was, but he'd discovered a long-lost friend. Hymie felt sure Mike would be able to shed some light on his questions, and if it was over a few jars for old times' sake then so much the better.

Murphy appeared a few minutes later and led Hymie around the corner for the promised drink.

Part Eleven

In the words of the late, great Irving Berlin, "There may be trouble ahead, but while there's moonlight and music and love and romance...", yowza, yowza, yowza!! Love and romance may be on the ropes but giving oneself up to wild uninhibited pleasure was still as fashionable as ever and certainly on the agenda for Janis Turner, or "Steffie" as we have come to know her.

First, however, she had to get rid of Hymie Goldman. He had always been disposable, like a soiled nappy, but it had suited her to leave him bumbling around in his ineffectual manner. He was becoming a bore and that would never do.

She pressed the keypad on her mobile and dialled the ex-directory number of a certain Master Lau. He was poor value as an entertaining after-dinner speaker, but he knew how to eradicate vermin.

In his tenth-floor apartment the phone began to ring. The King of Evil was home for the evening.

"Lau."

"Just listen. I understand you are in the market for a golden pig. My partner will meet you at Benny's Unbeatable Bakery on the Finchley Road at eleven a.m. tomorrow."

"Who is this?"

"Be there," she barked, then rang off.

Where was that useless waster Tony Lee? He'd better keep out of her way for a long, *long* time, unless he wanted to look like a portrait by Picasso. The deal was, he would meet her at the roulette wheel at eleven p.m., arrange for the little ball to stop on three pre-arranged numbers and they would split the proceeds. Even as she cursed him, Tony Lee was lying facedown in a nameless alley with his throat slit.

She took a cab to her favourite dance club.

"Leptospirosis!"

"I've never heard of it, love. Sounds like a bacterial infection in rabbits."

"You're not as dumb as you look, are you?" she quipped.

"Thanks. I think, but what a stupid name for a nightclub. Whatever happened to the Palais or the Tower Ballroom? Things never get better anymore, they just get weirder!"

"Do you want the fare or not, dog-breath?"

"Yes, God help me, I want the fare. So where are we going?" he enquired, cagily.

"Just off the Finchley Road. I'll show you when we get there."

The yellow cab trundled off down the road. Twenty minutes passed in brooding silence, before Steffie spoke again.

"This will do."

The cab pulled up in front of a neon-lit sweatbox. She climbed out and passed the driver a banknote.

"Don't go spending it all at once, honey," she teased.

"Take it easy, lady." He felt like he had just released a leopard from his taxi.

"I always do," purred Steffie.

She ascended the cast-iron spiral staircase at the front of the building in a few athletic leaps, pushed through the swing doors unchecked and bounded into the club like a coiled spring eager to unwind. Passing through the doors she was quickly devoured by the bright lights, body heat and pulsating high-energy dance music.

On the dance floor she became another person; a lithe and powerful force of nature, which neither beat nor rhythm could control. She knew exactly what she wanted and exactly how to get it.

Steffie gyrated across the floor in ever wider circles around her handbag, while the butt of her favourite handgun began to rub against her inner thigh, sending her all too soon into paroxysms of pleasure.

"Oooooooooooooh! aaaaaaaaaaaaah!!"

"Who said dancing wasn't as good as sex?" she murmured to herself.

A guy in his twenties stood before her, virtually drooling at the sight of her aroused body.

"Not me, goddess," he said with a smile.

"Are you talking to me, pretty boy?" She was laughing at him. Man as predator had no meaning for her.

"If the cap fits, wear it, I always say," he continued, with practised ease.

"Do you always come on so strong, honey?"

"Only when I like what I see." It seemed to him that his luck was definitely in.

"Good, then follow me."

She winked at him in slow motion and watched his self-assurance crumble, then led him by his bootlace tie into the ladies' toilet, pulled him into a cubicle after her then slammed and locked the door behind him.

"Show me what you can do, honey."

They kissed, a long slow passionate kiss that left him gasping for air, and caressed, gently at first but with mounting sensuality, until his senses were engulfed in the tidal wave of her desire. He ceased to be a person and became an object of self-gratification, rising and falling in the age-old choreography of sex. He became exhausted, she, momentarily at least, fulfilled.

"Wow! What's your name?" he asked, dazzled.

"I don't use names, lover," she smiled.

"If I give you my number will you call me?"

"Only *asshole*."

As a boy he had been advised to shun the frumious bandersnatch, and now he knew why. There was no pleasing some people.

"Come on, lover."

She led him out of the cubicle and back into the club by the remains of his shirt collar. His clothes bore their dishevelled state like a badge of male pride; he had conquered this lioness of lust, though he knew in his heart she had conquered him.

"Hang on, babe," he said, struggling to keep up.

"I'll have a double brandy, with some crushed nuts…I mean ice," she smiled, playfully. He was a *nice* boy really, the kind you could take home to meet mother, fifty years or so ago. It wouldn't do, of course – just one complication too many.

He walked dutifully to the bar to get her drink, while she walked out onto the top of the spiral staircase. She looked up at the stars wistfully for a moment. We were never really free, she thought sadly; not like shooting stars in the great infinity of space, just so many birds in a gilded cage, hoping for the chance to spread our wings. Freedom came at a price, a price she would pay come what may. It was time to dispense with her alter ego; Janis Turner, and anyone who had ever known her.

Part Twelve

The Pink Parrot was *the* definitive example of late '80s barroom décor. You took a perfectly respectable pub, ripped its insides out and festooned it with fifty-year-old gardening implements. The *pièce de resistance* was a mock-up of the bonnet and bumper of a 1950s Caddy, which some public-spirited soul appeared to have driven clean through the wall above the bar. Clearly it didn't pay to drink and drive. As if the décor wasn't sufficiently challenging, the piped music was loud enough to wake the dead, as a quick glance at the clientèle readily confirmed.

Their scrupulous host no doubt felt sufficiently concerned about the level of bar prices to dream up a list of names for his cocktails, fit to adorn the children of A-list celebrities. It was clearly essential to divert his clients' attention from the second mortgage required to imbibe.

Mike and Hymie sat on their chromium-plated barstools and looked down the drinks list for a laugh.

"What's it to be, Mike, a Brooklyn Sunrise or a Madison Marvel? No, wait, what's this? How about a Yachtsman's Willy?"

"No thanks, mate, this place is already giving me the willies. I thought we came in here for a drink," said Mike. "Do you serve beer in here, sunshine?" he enquired.

The barman looked at him as though he were a visitor from another planet, or something unpleasant he had found attached to the sole of his shoe.

"*Beer*, sir? This is a cocktail bar. All we have is there on the list."

"Let me see now...we'll have a couple of Dental Drills and help yourself to a Big Greeny on me," said Hymie.

"A Big Greeny, sir?"

"Just my little joke. We'll be sitting at that corner table over there," he said, pointing.

"So, you've got your own firm of private investigators, Artie. Any money in it?"

"Do I look like there is?" queried Hymie. "Incidentally, I've changed my name for business reasons."

"What business reasons? Have you done a runner with the VAT?"

Hymie appeared to be considering it momentarily as a new source of income, before coming clean. "I don't *earn* enough to charge VAT...although the clients won't know that I suppose."

"What name do you use now then? Albert Finckelstein?" asked Mike.

"Close. Hymie Goldman."

"And are you any good?"

"I get by. How about yourself, Mike? What have you been up to for the last twenty years?"

"A bit of this, a bit of that and a bit of the other...you know how it is."

He knew exactly how it was. You did what you could and lived on dreams of a bright tomorrow.

"I'm working on a big case right now. It could set me up for life."

"Sounds good. I could use some extra cash if you need an extra pair of hands."

"I can't pay you until the case is solved, but I'm meeting a representative from the Total Disaster Insurance Corporation tomorrow. Perhaps you could join me?"

"You're kidding me, what kind of insurance company would call itself that? Still, if it's on the level, I'd be glad to, Art...sorry, Hymie. As long as there's a decent few quid in me kick at the end of the case. I'm a night worker, so the days are usually quiet. Where do they hail from, the Total Disaster guys?"

"America apparently. We'll find out more tomorrow."

"When and where?" asked Mike, eager to close the deal.

"You know Benny Baker's place on the Finchley Road?"

Mike nodded.

"Well, it's there at eleven a.m."

"You're telling me you run an investigations agency from a fast food restaurant?"

"No, of course not, Mike, it's just neutral territory."

"Why, are they trying to kill you, these insurance guys?"

"No, but I've had a bit of bother at the office lately so I thought I'd steer clear for a few days. How about you, Mike, have you been doing *security* work for long?"

"I was in the army for twelve years; the Gunners."

"You're not still an Arsenal supporter are you?"

"Of course! Well, you can't be in the Royal Artillery, grow up in North London and support *Chelsea*, can you?" he grimaced.

"At least Chelsea have the occasional British player, it's like going to watch a United Nations' eleven at Highbury," complained Hymie.

"Highbury? Jeez, where have you been, Goldman? It's called the Emirates Stadium these days."

"Yeah, that's because you have to be an oil sheikh to afford the ticket prices. I miss the old days though. You know, my granddad used to tell me he saw England beat Italy at Highbury in 1934, when there were seven Arsenal players in the *England* team!"

"I know; I am a true supporter, you know, although I admit I probably wouldn't believe you otherwise, H. Anyway, as I was saying, I was with the old *ubique quo fas et Gloria ducunt*..."

"Who're you calling a cu...?"

"...boys for twelve years. Save it, H. There's nothing funny about being in the army. Eventually I got fed up of taking orders from cocky young upstarts who didn't know their epaulets from their elbow and decided not to re-enlist. Since then I've been throwing people out of a succession of nightclubs. It ain't a bad crack really, or at least it wasn't until the Triads moved in and used the clubs to front their drug pushing. That doesn't sit too well with me, see. I've seen what drugs can do to kids and it ain't pretty."

"How do you know about the drugs?"

"I'm not blind. They have couriers going back and forth all the time. They do a good job and don't ask questions and they stick around, otherwise they don't last long," explained Mike.

"Say, there was something I meant to ask you," said Hymie. "That girl you were talking to at the club earlier..."

"Steffie?"

"That's the one."

"Have you taken a good look at yourself in a mirror lately, H? You'd have no chance."

"Very funny. No, I wondered if you knew her surname, as she looks familiar."

"Part of the case you're working on?" asked Mike.

"Could be," remarked Hymie, noncommittally.

"Sorry, H, I don't know her last name, I just know her as Steffie. She's as smart as paint though...lovely girl."

"Do you know who she was after at the club?"

"A guy named Tony Lee, a croupier. I haven't seen him lately though."

"Thanks for the gen," said Hymie appreciatively.

"No worries. Does it help?"

"It's too...early to tell." Hymie paused to reconsider his words. Were the cocktails beginning to take their toll, or was it the cumulative effect of sleep deprivation and poor diet?

It looked like Janis or Steffie Scarlatti, as she probably was, had been in cahoots with this guy Tony Lee, one of the croupiers at the club. Something had happened to him as he hadn't shown up and people rarely failed to show up for Steffie.

"So tell me about this case you're working on, H."

"I'd be happy to tell you, Mike, but first you'll have to sign the Official Secrets Act in triplicate...oh, go on then, buy me another drink and we'll call it quits. Make mine a U-Bend...easy on the mara...chino sherries, and have one yourshelf."

The booze, credit and bull flowed freely as Hymie shared his recent life story, theories and aspirations with his old friend.

"Well, you never could hold your drink," said Mike at the end of the session, bundling the inebriated investigator into a passing taxi. "What kind of detective are you anyway?" he asked.

"The old-fasshioned kind that never sholves cases and shpends mosht of his shpare time in hoshpital," he slurred.

"I'll see you at Benny's tomorrow morning at eleven, Hymie," said Mike, waving him off. "Let's hope you've sobered up by then, or the insurance company will think we're a couple of right Charlies!"

Part Thirteen

The following morning the papers were full of the suspicious death of the croupier Tony Lee, found by an unfortunate dustman with his throat slit (the croupier, not the dustman). News being what it is, a competitive process, he managed only page seven of *The Times*, but he made the front page of the *Hendon and Finchley Times*, with photos, and an editorial on the decline into gangland violence of large parts of North London. Sensationalism sold papers, especially in Hendon and Finchley, where it made a welcome change from tedium.

In her luxuriously appointed first-floor apartment Steffie Scarlatti cut out the column inches devoted to the murder of Tony Lee and pasted them into her scrapbook. So, she hadn't *actually* wielded the knife this time, but he was surely dead because of her. She kept a grisly record of all her killings like an actor collecting rave reviews.

Meanwhile, Hymie Goldman sat in the grottiest flat he'd ever seen, and he was something of an authority, drinking black coffee and reading the *Finchley News*. Lee's death would have made more of an impression had he been less hungover.

"You sure you didn't know Tony Lee, H?"

"Poor slob, no. I never met the guy. Got any orange juice, Mike?"

"Never use the stuff."

"What time is it?" asked Hymie. His own watch had been broken for months, though he still wore it to suggest punctuality.

"Nearly ten."

"We'd better be making tracks if we're going to keep that appointment."

"I'll ring for a cab," said Mike, lifting the receiver.

"'Ello dere, man, Ramjam Taxis here, weir jawanago?"

"My name's Murphy and I want a cab from 62 Swanswell Road to Benny's Bakery on the Finchley Road – pronto, Tonto."

"Fiftine minutes, mon."

Mike slammed down the phone. There was only one thing worse than taking a cab in London – public transport. Hymie was beginning to regret parting with the Zebaguchi 650. It hadn't been from choice. He'd somehow neglected to ask Janis for the keys back at their last meeting. He didn't even know exactly where it was, but it was too late now.

Half an hour later the "cab" arrived. They heard it before they saw it; the sound intimated that a well-attended reggae concert was being held in a nearby park, by the legendary Bob Marley. The volume seemed to grow exponentially from just south of Zion and then a black R-reg BMW 3 series pulled up outside. It had clearly been a quality car in its day, but its day had been and gone. Try telling that to its owner, Elroy Moses Zachariah Smith III; a fully paid-up member of the cabbie subculture who lived by just three golden rules: keep no written records, always arrive ten minutes late, and most important of all, "be cool".

"Hey mon, getta move on, you're wastin' my gas!" said Elroy Smith, uninhibited by any notion of customer service.

Mike toyed briefly with the idea of beating the crap out of him but then remembered that this would necessitate a trip on public transport and thought better of it.

Hymie noticed that one of the cab's electric windows seemed to be freaking out – flying up and down at will – but like his friend before him decided that beggars couldn't be choosers.

"Ehh man, is your name Murty?" asked Smith.

"No, Murphy."

"Murty, Murphy, whaddever…dats it, git in de car!"

They climbed into the back of the cab. The cabbie put his foot down and they sped off to join the nearest traffic jam. Every time the car stood idling in traffic for a few minutes the faulty electric window seemed to suck in every noxious exhaust fume for miles around, so that they were glad to bail out at journey's end.

They paid him off and he passed them a dog-eared business card.

"See you agin mon."

"Not if I see you first, sunshine!" said Mike, through clenched teeth.

They arrived at Benny Baker's place with five minutes to spare so seated themselves in the restaurant section within sight of the entrance.

"Morning, boys, what can I get you today?" It was the proprietor himself.

"Hi, Ben, this is my old mate from schooldays, Mike."

"Pleased to meet you, Mike."

"Two teas and two of your breakfast specials should do the trick, Ben."

"Cash?"

"If you can spare any," quipped Hymie. Mike nodded his assent.

"Coming right up."

While the waitress made up their order Benny took off his apron and crossed to the other side of the counter for a chat.

"How's the case going, H? Made any progress?"

"Fair to middlin', Ben. Did you get a visit from the boys in blue?"

"Yeah, some vicious-looking sergeant called Terse. He wanted to know if I knew you and whether I knew where you were."

"And you said?"

"Oh, you know, I just told him I knew you by sight, that you came in the bakery from time to time and I hadn't seen you recently."

"And that was it? He left?" asked Hymie, incredulously.

"Pretty much; at least, the police circus on your doorstep moved out of town, but I'm sure I've seen a few more plain-clothed detectives around than usual."

Suddenly the party was over.

It was one of those "JFK assassination" moments, where years later, those present remembered every last detail of where they had been and what they had been doing. Even if they did choose to embellish.

As the clock on the wall struck eleven there was an almighty explosion.

BOOM CRACKA THOOM!! KABABOOM!!!

The front of the restaurant imploded into a gigantic fireball. The plate glass windows shattered into a million splinters, flying in all directions, the frames melted and warped. Mike hit the deck first, pulling his friend and their host to the ground with consummate skill and practised ease. It was a timely manoeuvre, as no sooner had the glass fallen than the front of the bakery was deluged with wave upon wave of machine-gun fire. The noise was apocalyptic. Everywhere tables, chairs and catering equipment were torn asunder and scattered far and wide. Nothing moved in the carnage.

Suddenly, Hymie became aware of a pulsing sensation in his trouser pocket. His mobile phone, which was never switched on, must have been activated when he hit the floor.

"Hello, Mr Goldman, Sarah Chandar speaking. I wondered if you had had time to reconsider my outline proposal for your business?"

"Yes...er, no, I'm afraid you'll have to excuse me, Sarah, I'm a little busy right now." He switched her and his mobile off.

Alarms sounded upstairs and in the neighbouring premises. In short order police, fire engines and ambulances started to arrive. The army of hell-raisers responsible for the atrocity seemed to have just melted away.

"I don't think they were from the Total Disaster Insurance Corporation," said Hymie.

"If they were, they certainly lived up to their name," rejoined Mike.

Benny was in too much pain to talk, having taken a deflected bullet to the shoulder. He was escorted away to Edgware General in an ambulance with a couple of his staff. Mercifully there had been only one fatality, a regular customer of eighty-three, whose arteries were too hardened to allow for fast evasive action. Mike and Hymie miraculously suffered only minor injuries, though Mike was removing fragments of broken glass from his hair for days afterwards.

The restaurant looked like it had lost a fight with Lennox Lewis. Restaurants rarely faced such tough opposition.

"Is there something you haven't been telling me, Hymie?" asked Mike. "It's becoming clear that some heavy-duty villains really don't like you. Who have you upset?"

"Where do I begin? Old Mrs Timmins, Sergeant Terse and Inspector Decca, Janis Turner, the whole of the North London criminal fraternity…"

"The Triads?"

"Well, I'm not exactly on their Christmas list, but this is a bit much."

"Mr Goldman! I'd been wondering when we'd be seeing you again."

"Hello, Inspector. Good of you to drop by. This is my friend, Mike Murphy. Mike, this is Inspector Ray Decca, known to his friends as Clueless…sorry, *Cluedo*."

"Well, it's lucky for you we *were* passing, sunshine, or you'd be pushing up daisies by now."

"Very kind, I'm sure."

"No trouble. Now, I'm sure you gents will both be only too happy to join me down at the station for a little chat, because you're both decent law-abiding citizens who would hate to be accused of obstructing the course of justice."

"Or any other trumped-up charges he can think of," murmured Hymie.

"You what, Goldman?"

"Nothing…nothing, Inspector."

They were escorted into the back of an unmarked police car and driven away to Finchley Road Police Station. Conversation dried up as Hymie tried to work out what he should and shouldn't tell Decca, and Mike wondered what on earth he had allowed himself to get involved in. Time alone would tell.

Part Fourteen

The place: police interview room one, Finchley Road nick; the time: later that day. Hymie Goldman sat staring into space as usual. On the other side of the desk, Inspector Ray Decca was trying hard not to lose his patience.

"Stop the tape, Reidy. When I want to hear *Book at Bedtime* I'll switch on Radio Four. You *have* heard, I suppose, of wasting police time, Goldman?"

Hymie smiled the kind of smile that implied it was one of his hobbies.

PC Reidy, who had been on the verge of mastering the ancient art of sleeping through a witness interview, sat bolt upright in his chair, reached over to the Taiwanese cassette recorder and pressed the pause button.

"I've a good mind to charge you for it at that, Goldman, failing first degree murder of course. Incidentally, we've noticed that the incidence of motoring offences has dropped significantly of late. Have you sold your car?"

"I haven't seen my car for a few days, it's true…my assistant, Janis, had it last, but as for the murder, give me a break! You ought to be out there trying to catch the scum that destroyed Benny's Bakery, not hauling me over the coals for something I clearly never did. I nearly got *killed*…or do you think that was just an elaborate suicide attempt?!"

"Reidy, switch the ruddy tape *on!*"

"I want to see my solicitor," said Hymie.

"So do we – he jumped bail on a fraud charge six months ago."

"I wondered who that postcard from Alicante was from."

"Are you ready to tell us what you know, or would you like to spend a few more hours in the cells?" asked Decca, dismissively.

"Okay, I'll tell you what I know. It isn't much. The way my life's going at the moment, police protection is better than nothing. Is there any news of Benny Baker?"

"He's stable. He'll be fine in a few weeks."

"Good. Right, where shall I begin?"

"At the *beginning.*"

Down the corridor in interview room two, Sergeant Barry Terse was applying all his ingenuity to the task of interviewing Mike Murphy.

"You did it, didn't you?"

"I don't understand the question. Was it a question, Sergeant?"

"You know damn well what I'm talking about. You killed Lee and destroyed Benny's Bakery to make it look like a gangland killing."

"Yes, that's right, you're too smart for me. I should have known I was no match for your *clever* interview techniques."

"Blast it! Switch on the recorder *now*, Potter!"

Mike's tongue had talked him into as many scrapes as his fists had fought him out of. Usually he was big enough and ugly enough to get out on the side of the angels, but Barry Terse was built along the same lines. His response to heavy sarcasm was a smack in the mouth and he administered it before Mike had time to reflect that winding up coppers in a police station was a mug's game. Murphy reeled back in his seat, bounced off the wall and leapt to his feet brandishing what was left of the interview-room chair.

"Switch *off* the tape, Potter!"

In the Mexican standoff that ensued, Terse and Potter prepared to overpower their desperate witness, while the latter came belatedly to his senses.

"Happy birthday, Sergeant," he said, handing the chair fragments across the desk to Terse with a broad grin.

He wasn't going to give them the pleasure.

Back down the other end of the corridor Hymie was warming to the task of spilling the beans. He could easily have become a confirmed bean bunger.

"...that's all I know about Lucy Scarlatti," he said, a few minutes later. "She was my client for three wonderful days before she died in a hail of bullets. As I said, she hired me to recover some memento of mainly sentimental value her sister had stolen from their dead father."

"A pig?"

"Well, I don't like to speak ill of the dead, but he wasn't very popular, apparently."

"No, the memento – was it a statue of a pig?" asked Decca.

"Yes, so she said."

"Not a diary?" continued Decca.

"No, different things entirely…pigs, pink and fat with a leg at each corner, diaries, small and rectangular, made of pulped wood," quipped Hymie, ill-advisedly.

"But last time we met, Goldman, you told me she was trying to recover her father's diary, as it contained a treasure map."

Hymie smiled sheepishly. "Ah, yes…sorry, I wasn't feeling well at the time."

"So let's get this story straight, you went to visit your client on the night she died?"

"Yes."

"Alone? Or with someone else?"

"With my assistant, Janis Turner."

"Again, Mr Goldman, that's not what you told me earlier. You said you were alone."

"Well, she stayed in the car so in a sense she wasn't really there."

"It's you who's not all there, Goldman."

"I have reason to believe that Janis Turner and Steffie Scarlatti are one and the same person and that she murdered her sister; my client, Lucy Scarlatti," said Hymie.

"Over a statuette of a pig?"

"Yes."

"Not over a diary with a treasure map in it?"

"No."

"You're sure?" asked Decca. "You don't want to change your story just one more time?"

"Yes…I mean no…I mean yes and no," said Hymie, confused.

"Okay, tell me again, what happened on the night of the murder?" Decca felt like he was making progress at last.

"Janis Turner, aka Steffanie Scarlatti, and I drove over to Lucy Scarlatti's apartment," repeated Hymie.

"In *your* car?"

"Yes. The Zebaguchi 650."

"Never heard of it," said Decca. "What's the registration number?"

"R256 HOG."

"Colour?"

"Mainly silver."

"And what was the address you drove to?" Decca was nothing if not thorough.

"Riverside Drive...over in Docklands," hesitated Hymie, "but I can't remember the number offhand."

"But you've previously identified it as number 35," added Decca. "And when you got there, what happened?"

"I've told you, Inspector, I went into the flat to tell my client I hadn't made any progress with the case and that she was wasting her money..."

"A pity you didn't tell her that the first time you met; she may still be alive."

"...and then, and then...I don't know. I remember, some time later, hearing she was dead and that I'd been shot; as if I needed telling, but I couldn't recall what happened at the time. I heard these things after I came to in hospital."

"So you have no idea who killed Lucy Scarlatti?"

"All I remember is my client's last word, 'Steffanie'!"

"Just that?"

"Just that."

"And what happened to Janis Turner aka Steffie Scarlatti?"

"She told me she drove away, but I don't have any evidence for that and if she did, I don't know when she left or where she went."

"Do you think she killed Lucy Scarlatti, Mr Goldman?"

"Yes. She had the motive, the opportunity and the inclination. She gunned down a professional hit man only the day before."

"You saw her kill Chiu Mann?"

"*Chiu Mann?* Was that his name? He was barely human; a vicious killing machine. Incredibly I didn't catch his name as he was trying to cut me into little pieces with a ruddy great sword at the time."

"Did you ever meet Tony Martino?" pressed Decca.

"What is this, twenty questions, Inspector? No, I never met him, should I have?"

"He had been murdered by Chiu Mann shortly before you arrived at the scene."

"In that case, I did meet the poor slob...although he was already dead at the time," explained Hymie.

"What were you doing there?"

"I've always wanted to see South Mimms."

"Goldman! Just get on with it," Decca snapped.

"My client gave me the address. She said it was the last address she had for her sister Steffanie."

"You went alone?"

"Yes, but I was followed by Janis," surmised Hymie.

"Did you ever find the pig statuette?"

"No."

"Stop the tape, Reidy. Thank you, Mr Goldman. If you'd told me all this earlier you might not be looking at a charge of obstructing a police investigation."

Decca stood up and left the room. Back in his office he rang through to interview room two for Terse to join him.

"So, Terse, what have you got for me?"

"Got 'im bang to rights, Chief...with a little judicious editing of course."

"Terse, you disappoint me."

"He practically confessed to killing the Chink, Tony Lee."

"*Practically*, Terse? How exactly 'practically'?"

"Well 'e took a little reminding, sir."

"I thought as much. Do something for me, Sergeant."

"Chief?"

"See if you can locate a car. It's a silver Zebaguchi 650, registration R256 HOG."

"You havin' me on, Chief?"

"No, Terse, get on with it, man!"

The inspector decided he would have to take over the cross-examination of the other witness in person.

"Hello, Mr Murphy, I'd like to ask you a few questions."

"Ask all you like, mate, but I doubt if I'll know the answers. I hadn't seen Hymie for twenty years until we bumped into each other last night."

"So, your luck's taken a turn for the worse, I see."

"You could say that. I see my share of trouble as a doorman at the Rainbow Rooms, but no one ever tried to blow me up until this morning."

"Well, that's the price of associating with Hymie Goldman, Mr Murphy."

Mike's eyebrows knitted into a frown as though he found the words difficult to accept. "What happened to Sergeant Dipstick?" he asked.

"Look, if you're going to be abusive, I'll stop the interview and leave you to cool off in the cells for an hour, but if you've got any sense you'll stop trying to be smart and answer my questions. Right?"

Murphy looked blankly at Decca, before nodding, almost imperceptibly.

"If you work at the Rainbow Rooms you must have known Tony Lee?"

"Not to talk to, no. He was a croupier and those guys think they're above talking to doormen."

"When did you last see him alive?"

"Weeks ago...I dunno exactly," said Mike.

"Can you think of anyone who may have wanted to kill him?"

"No, but like I said, I didn't know him *that* well."

"Where were you last night?"

"Down the club till about eleven, then I went for a drink with Hymie Goldman."

"And where did you go for your drink?"

"The Pink Parrot."

"Did anyone try to get in touch with Lee over the last few days?"

"Only Steffie."

"Steffie?" quizzed Decca, suddenly interested.

"Yeah, a friend of his," explained Mike. "I think they used to work together."

"What was her surname?"

"I couldn't tell you."

"Describe her for me, then," asked the inspector.

"Tall, maybe five-foot ten. A looker; brunette with long legs and a smile that would stop traffic."

"Thank you, Mr Murphy. If you'll just sign the statement that PC Potter has prepared, then you're free to go."

"What about Hymie?" blurted Mike.

"He should be out shortly if you'd care to wait."

So saying Decca returned to his prime suspect with a heavy heart. It looked like the imbecile Goldman was telling him the truth. Still, he could have him for obstruction any time he wanted.

"Okay, Reidy, start the tape. Interview with Hymie Goldman resumed at 4.50 p.m. Just a few more questions, Mr Goldman. Can you think of any reason why Janis Turner, or for sake of argument let's call her Steffie Scarlatti, would want to murder Tony Lee?"

"They were working a numbers racket at the Rainbow Rooms' casino, only Lee failed to show up," said Hymie, wondering how long the questions would last. "Janis, or rather Steffie, seemed surprised when he failed to keep their appointment, so I assume someone else killed him. Besides, the papers said he was found with his throat slit and that's not her m-o; she's a firearms fanatic."

"What do you know about the numbers racket, Goldman?"

"Not a lot. All I know is that someone rang my office a couple of times, shouted out three pairs of numbers, which, before you ask, I can't remember, and hung up," said Hymie. "Adding two and two together to make five, I assumed the call was for my assistant, Janis Turner, aka Steffie, who as it turns out knew the croupier Tony Lee. She went to see him at the casino on the night I ran into Mike Murphy at the Rainbow Rooms."

"Thank you, what you say does seem to fit the facts as we know them. That will do for now, you're free to go as soon as you've signed your statement. We'll be in touch about the parking fines. Oh, and Goldman…"

"Inspector?"

"Don't leave London unless I give you permission first, *right*?"

"Of course not. Besides, I'd need to borrow the fare first." Were they really letting him go? He wasn't sure whether to laugh or cry. Since it had never occurred to him that they would release him, he didn't have the first idea of what to do next.

Outside at the desk he was reunited with Mike.

"You okay, H?"

"Yes thanks, Mike. I feel as though a great weight has been lifted off my shoulders and I have a craving for pizza."

"I'll join you...but it won't be Benny's."

A pained look flitted across Hymie's face. "It looks like we have another score to settle," he said.

Part Fifteen

The Prince of Darkness was just settling down in his favourite pink velour armchair to watch his favourite game show, *The Price Is All Wrong*, with a nice hot cup of cocoa when the phone started ringing in the hall.

He toyed with the idea of ignoring it, but he simply *couldn't* do it. For an ex-directory number it seemed to get far too many calls. He had gone ex-directory many years before on discovering that his name, P Lau, was an open invitation to small-minded pranksters to call him up and ask him if he had prawn balls. What was the matter with people in this country? Pilau rice was Indian, not Chinese. Were they stupid or what? It was some small consolation to him to know that those who crossed him generally found themselves on the wrong side of the great divide.

"Lau."

"Hello, Mr Lau, Mrs Timmins here. I've got a bone to pick with you. You promised me faithfully you'd get rid of that awful man Goldman and I have it on reliable authority that he was released from Finchley Road Police Station not ten minutes ago."

"But my dear Mrs Timmins..."

"Don't give me the old soft soap, Lau. When I pay good money I expect the best service available. You gave me your word they'd be scraping him off the pavement within twenty-four hours. What kind of hit service are you running?"

"I'll look into it, Mrs T. Rest assured no effort will be spared to ensure matters are put straight at the earliest opp…"

"I hope you're right, Lau. When I think of the way that dreadful man caused the death of my prize pussy Tiddles, my blood runs cold. Of course I have Cedric now…"

"Cedric?"

"My blue macaw; a lovely bird, but it's just not the same. I want results, Lau, not wind and piffle. Do I make myself clear?"

She hung up on him, leaving the Prince of D feeling not a little foolish and somewhat incensed, both at the nerve of the woman, and more alarmingly at the ineptitude of his hit squad. They had only to eliminate a complete idiot, a job he could have done himself with his eyes closed. You just couldn't get good help these days, he reflected sadly.

He descended in the lift to his office on the first floor and dug out the "contracts pending" file. There it was, in black and white, contract 207:

> To: Termination of one H Goldman of 792A Finchley Road, £5,000 plus travel expenses, 48 hour priority service.

Everything seemed to be in order, except that the party of the third part was still walking the streets of North London.

There was a file note adding that a woman had called to notify him that H Goldman was in possession of the golden pig. Not likely. Perhaps that was why they hadn't finished the job, though again that didn't seem at all likely. However, as they hadn't located it yet, anything was possible. It was time for a little chat with Mr Hymie Goldman. He lifted the receiver and made a few calls.

Hymie, who for once was walking around with a spring in his step and a smile on his face, had developed a deep loathing for Edgware General Hospital. In their short acquaintance he had been interrogated by the fuzz, fallen down a laundry chute and nearly been poisoned there – though the latter could just have been a paranoid delusion triggered by the effects of the NHS cuts on the canteen.

He went there now to pay his respects to Benny Baker, from a combination of genuine concern and a guilty conscience.

"How is he, nurse?"

"Suffering from severe shock, I'm afraid. A delayed reaction like that is quite common in trauma cases like his. Someone destroyed his restaurant, you know, while he was in it. He may not recognise you...are you family?" she enquired.

"...yes, er, I'm his brother Sydney from Australia," bluffed Hymie. When called upon for a spontaneous response, all originality deserted him.

"Mr Baker, your brother Sydney has come to visit you," said the nurse.

"I don't have a brother Sydney."

"Poor man...don't expect too much of him, Sydney."

"Thank you, nurse," added Hymie, politely.

She walked off down the ward leaving the two *brothers* to talk.

"How are you, Syd? How's the family?" asked Benny. He was suffering from a form of amnesia that had genuinely erased Hymie like a virus from the hard drive of his mind.

"It's me, Ben...Hymie, I've brought you some grapes and a get well card."

"Sorry I didn't recognise you, Ben-Hymie old chap, it's this condition I've got, I'm not even sure who *I* am half the time."

"Ben, watch my lips, it's *me*...Hymie Goldman, your mate."

"Do you still have your own business?"

"Of course I do, we were only talking about it a few days ago."

"I hear there's a terrible recession in Melbourne...it must be affecting you."

"Not so as you'd notice...my office is in Finchley."

"It's okay, Syd, don't worry. I know things haven't been

exactly rosy between you and Joyce. She's at that *funny* age when all you can do is grit your teeth and hold on tight for the ride."

"He's better off out of it," thought Hymie. "There's a homicidal maniac roaming the streets and the pizza king of North London thinks I'm his long lost brother Syd from Australia. That just takes the ruddy biscuit. How do I get a delusion of my own, God? Anything to get out of here!"

Hymie collected Mike from the waiting room and they took the lift down to the hospital's main entrance.

"I know they let us walk out of that nick as free men, but I'm not daft enough to think that we're out of the woods yet, Mike."

"Well, it's been nice catching up, Hymie. There's never a dull moment with you around, but I need to get back to my own life again. I may not own my own business but at least I've got the flat, three square meals a day, a job I can do standing on my head and footy on a Saturday." Mike held out a hand like a bunch of bananas for Hymie to shake goodbye.

In just a few short hours Hymie had come to rely on his old friend, the man mountain, and the thought of trying to solve the case without him seemed almost unbearable.

"Well, that *is* a shame, Mike," he said. "I was so impressed with the way you handled things at Benny's Bakery that I was thinking of inviting you to join the business."

"It's good of you to offer, Hymie, but if the last forty-eight hours are anything to go by I'd need some serious danger money to get involved in *your* business. What were you going to offer me? Equal partnership?"

Hymie, who had had no such thought, struggled to find words. "Ahem, well, I was, er...thinking more of, ah...but of course, a *junior* partnership would be something to consider, eh? After all, there are people interested in buying this business," added Hymie, rashly.

"Oh, well, I'd *definitely* need to be a partner then. Otherwise, what job security would I have?"

Caught between a rock and a hard place, Hymie could neither face running the business single-handed, nor give any of it away while there was a chance of cashing in for megabucks. He wondered if the sight of his office might dampen Mike's enthusiasm for partnership.

"*I* know," said Hymie. "If we go back to the office, you can see for yourself what it means to be a partner, and if you're still interested in joining the firm we can negotiate the terms then and there."

"Sounds fair," said Mike. "We may even be able to work out how to solve this case."

Hymie smiled. If there *was* a solution to the case, then together they would surely find it.

Part Sixteen

It was late, one or two a.m., when they arrived at the prestigious offices of JP Confidential. The plaque on the wall outside just said "792A", as if anything further would have been superfluous. The way things had been going lately, Hymie was convinced that it *didn't* pay to advertise.

Leading the way, Hymie crept up the staircase, signalling to Mike to be as quiet as possible. His caution was born of his now habitual fear that whatever *could* go wrong almost certainly *would.* The list of things that could go wrong seemed to stretch out to infinity, beginning with eviction from his office-cum-flat and ending with another attempt on his life. He had no illusions that he had been anything other than lucky thus far.

He searched his pockets for the office key with a growing sense of frustration. A small pile of detritus accumulated on the floor before him as he extracted fuse wire, paper handkerchiefs, a part-sucked boiled sweet, paperclips and an old Swiss Army knife, but nothing vaguely resembling a key from his voluminous pockets. He was a past master at losing things. In a long and illustrious career he had lost keys, cars, car keys, money and clients. He'd even lost a wife once and that wasn't easy.

"Oh stuff this!" cried Mike, running at the door sideways on and hitting it at shoulder height with his full body weight.

There was a dreadful crunching sound.

"Mike!"

"Oh, don't tell me you've found the ruddy key, H!"

"No, it's not that."

"So?"

"That's not *my* office."

The big man looked crestfallen.

"Mine's next door, that one belongs to the opera singer."

"She doesn't *live* here I take it?" queried Mike.

"No, she just uses it as a rehearsal room."

Mike poked his head around the door, which was hanging forlornly by a solitary hinge.

"Do you think we should leave her a note or something?"

"Or something, definitely," said Hymie, uncharitably.

Mike shrugged. "She's your neighbour," he said. "So this one's yours," he added, turning the handle on the adjoining office door. It was open.

"That's odd. I'm sure it's never usually left open," said Hymie. "Unless, there's someone in there..."

"Don't be so ruddy paranoid, H. Nobody would break in to nick anything from a dump like this."

"Thanks. At least I'm self-employed, not like you... someone's hired help."

"Well at least I get paid regularly," said Mike.

He was clearly thinking back to life before JP Confidential.

They stood there in reception, bickering, when suddenly the lights came on.

"Good evening, gentlemen. So good of you to join me."

It was the crime boss, Lau.

They stared at him in disbelief. Behind and to the left and right of him, all dressed in martial arts gear and wearing red headbands, was his personal army. In suits and ties they could have passed for a Chinese international choir, but it was to hear Goldman sing that they had come to visit his office.

"You must excuse our unorthodox method of entry, Mr Goldman, but I was so anxious to meet you I could scarcely contain my enthusiasm. My name is Lau, Master Lau."

"Pleased to meet you," he said automatically, though he was clearly anything but.

"Whadda you want?" asked Mike, more abruptly. He could see that they were up against it and didn't see the point in playing games.

"I do *so* hope we can conduct matters in a civilised manner, Mr Goldman. I do *so* detest violence." He was toying with them. You didn't take a martial arts class on social visits at two in the morning.

"I couldn't agree more," said Hymie, with a sinking feeling in the pit of his stomach.

Resistance was futile, but at the same time life without resistance was no life at all.

"Perhaps you would care to leave us, Mr Murphy. This matter is no concern of yours."

"How do you know my name?"

"I know a good many things about you. As owner of the Rainbow Rooms I am also your employer."

Mike's granite-like features registered surprise in the exaggerated fashion of a silent movie star.

Hymie looked at him resignedly, but Mike, although many things, was neither a coward nor a deserter. "I'm not in any hurry to leave," he said.

"What's with the *army* then?" asked Hymie, nodding at Lau's confederates.

"These are merely some of my friends and associates who expressed a desire to meet you. We really have been most impressed by the way you have been handling the Scarlatti case," smarmed Lau, with grotesque politeness.

Incredulous but still flattered, Hymie smiled. "Is that why you're here?" he asked.

"Well, if Mr Murphy is *sure* he won't be running along then I will tell you. I have come to reclaim the statuette."

"Of the pig?"

"Naturally."

"I don't have it," said Hymie, as though that would end matters.

"You disappoint me, Mr Goldman. Perhaps it has only been luck after all that has kept you alive for so long. But I am sure I do you a disservice and you were about to add that you know where it is and are prepared to get it for me. You see, it really is very important to me that the statuette is returned to its rightful owner."

"And who might that be, Lau?"

"It is on a strictly need-to-know basis, Goldman, and you do not need to know. I assure you, however, that the knowledge would neither enlighten you, nor in any way enrich you, whereas concealing it will only cause you pain."

There was an underlying arrogance to Lau that really got up Hymie's nose. Mike felt the same way and had been looking for a soft spot to punch Lau's face in, but then reflected on the overwhelming odds against them and gave it up as a bad job. He settled for lifting JP Confidential's last remaining asset, the green plastic phone, off the floor and throwing it at Lau's head instead.

"Run for it!" shouted Mike.

Hymie, who was already on his back foot, immediately started heading for the staircase.

Lau ducked instantly but one of his henchmen received the phone fully in the face. "Ah so!" he cried, or it may have been something similar.

Mike dealt a couple of hefty blows to an approaching assailant, then followed Hymie's retreating path down the stairs.

It was only when they reached the foot of the stairs that they realised that the trap had been well and truly sprung, as a second troupe of martial arts enthusiasts filed in from the street, blocking their way.

"Resistance is futile, Goldman." It was the game show fanatic himself.

Lau descended the staircase and struck Mike across the face with a gloved hand. The latter flinched but didn't respond in kind.

"You have made your choice, Murphy. Take him away."

Mike was manhandled back upstairs into the office, where he was trussed and blindfolded.

Hymie followed under his own steam, the remaining hordes of henchmen parting before him like a latter day Sea of Galilee.

"What makes you think I have the pig, Lau?" asked Hymie.

"You were seen leaving a cottage in South Mimms on the day Chiu Mann was killed. I happen to know that he had gone there to collect the statuette from a petty thief who had stolen it," explained Lau.

"But I wasn't the only one there that day. There was a girl too, a girl called Steffanie Scarlatti. She shot Chiu Mann. She nearly killed me too. I still don't know why she didn't. If anyone has the pig, it's her. It certainly isn't me," insisted Hymie.

"A convenient story, Goldman, and not without strands of truth, I realise, but only to lend credibility to the basic lie at its heart. Let me suggest an alternative scenario: the very fact that a bungling pet investigator like yourself has been allowed to live so long by a professional killer like Ms Scarlatti suggests to me that you are either in thrall to her or in her employ, and as such you may be holding the statuette on her behalf." He was relentless. It was like facing the Spanish Inquisition.

Hymie still didn't know the whereabouts of the golden pig. Yes, he had removed it from the cottage in South Mimms, but he had kept it on his person until his final meeting with Lucy Scarlatti. When he'd woken up in hospital after her death it was missing and he'd assumed that Steffanie Scarlatti had reclaimed it.

"Well, if I find it, I'll let you know. Now, can we go, please?" said Hymie, with as much bravado as he could muster.

The Master of Doom nearly smiled – a dangerous pursuit as it would have cracked the mask of his face.

"Do you know what this statuette is worth, Goldman? Do you really think I would stop at anything to get it?"

"I dunno." With no prospect of its recovery, Hymie had begun to lose interest.

"It is a priceless religious artefact, removed from the Temple of Wei Ling in the early sixth century. Ever since then it has been sought for, fought for and coveted by some of the most powerful and ruthless men in the world. Your life would be snuffed out like a candle if the true owner even suspected that it was in your possession."

"Nice to know," said Hymie.

"Unless you assist me in its recovery, I very much fear that just such a thing may happen," said Lau with bogus concern.

"Look, I really don't have the thing. What do I have to do to prove it? You must have searched my office, right?"

"As you can probably imagine, Mr Goldman, the task of searching your office was not an onerous one. You appear to have no need of office furniture. I commend your abstinence."

"A mere misunderstanding with the bailiffs."

"Of course. Now perhaps you would like to join me at *my* premises to discuss the matter further."

"Well, I do have plans of my own," interjected Hymie, desperately trying to avoid the inevitable.

"But I insist."

"And Mr Murphy?"

"Will also be joining us for the dénouement."

"How could I refuse?" said Mike.

"Precisely," concluded Lau, ever one to have the last word.

A six o'clock news reporter was interviewing Inspector Ray Decca of the Metropolitan Police Force. Not that it mattered to many people, though his wife Sheila was impressed for once.

"Is there any truth in the rumours of a gang war on the streets of Finchley, Inspector?"

"We are currently investigating three suspicious deaths in the area, although there is no evidence to support that particular conclusion. We live in troubled times I'm afraid and only the efforts of our professional and dedicated police force prevent them from becoming more troubled."

"Can you tell us, Inspector, has anyone been arrested in connection with these murders?"

"Several people are helping us with our enquiries, though as yet no one has been charged. Clearly I would ask anyone watching to come forward to help us catch the killers if they have any information which may have a bearing on the case."

"So you are treating the murders as one related case?"

"We believe so, yes."

"Thank you, Inspector. Anyone watching who thinks they may have information which will assist the police should call 0845..."

Steffanie Scarlatti switched off the TV set and lit up a Havana cigar.

Police...what did they know? What did *anyone* know? She was invincible.

Here she was, sitting in her luxury West End apartment with a golden statuette of a pig resting in pride of place on the mantelpiece, having gunned down two people in as many weeks, and no one could touch her. She pulled out her handgun from the holster between her thighs and polished the barrel. It was a beauty, like herself, though she wasn't about to spoil her curves by wearing it in a shoulder holster. Men were so *crass*.

For months she had masqueraded as that gauche seventeen-year-old school-leaver Janis Turner, all to get revenge on her sister Lucretia, and no one had suspected a thing. Yes, she could simply have shot her or stolen the statuette, but it would have been so *obvious*. As it was, there was nothing to connect her with the pitiful Ms Turner. She had only to leave her clothes on the beach or in the wretched girl's digs with a suicide note to be free of her alter ego forever. Everything had gone to plan; Lucretia was dead now, and she had the statuette, though frankly it bored her. She valued only what she *didn't* have; her dead father's love, her next lover, the next kill, the next million dollars.

How tiresome the Triads were becoming. They had the local drugs racket all sewn up and that posturing old fool Lau was certainly heading for a fall. How sweet and fitting it would be for her to bring about his demise. He knew too much about her already and that would never do.

Part Seventeen

Master Lau was worried, *very* worried. He may have scaled the heights of the Triads, but no one was indispensable and he was getting old. Not *too* old, of course, but definitely more mature. He had become a little unfocused of late. Yes, he still got a mild thrill from inflicting death and destruction on the nameless masses, but to be honest, he'd rather be watching *The Price Is All Wrong, Which Box Holds The Dosh?*, or any of the other high-quality quiz shows on daytime TV.

As for that fiend in figure-hugging jeans, Steffanie Scarlatti, he was definitely of the view that she had outstayed her welcome. Unlike Goldman and Murphy, you couldn't just send her on her way with a salutary beating, safe in the knowledge that she would forever after keep her head below the parapet. She needed exterminating. That irked him. It wasn't that he objected to killing anyone per se, he just hated the increased police surveillance and reduced business takings that went with it.

Lau had always prided himself on the scrupulousness of his record-keeping. *Some people* argued that keeping records was a dangerous self-indulgence, but you had to have a hobby. Besides, he still planned to write his autobiography at the end of his career and achieve a kind of posthumous notoriety. There was no index-linked pension and retirement home in the Cotswolds to look forward to in his organisation, just the flash of silver and the taste of blood.

Business always came first with Lau. Drug baron Chang had insisted that the price for the forthcoming year's opium contract was the golden pig, and it had been non-negotiable. Since it now appeared that Ms Scarlatti was in possession of said porker, she must be eliminated and the pig recovered. It was that simple. For some strange reason *she* wanted Goldman dead, so the easiest route to her was through him. The beauty of silencing Goldman was that it also got that old bat Timmins off his back. It was hard to imagine what it was about the inconsequential detective that provoked such hostility, but it didn't actually matter.

It was easy enough to find Scarlatti; anyone whose calling card was a forty-five-calibre shell wasn't exactly the shy retiring type. He knew where to find her, but he wanted her to come to him. He had left a trail for her to follow, which led to Beachy Head and another gangland killing – of Goldman and Murphy. His only concern was the reliability of his own team. Their work of late left much to be desired, resulting in an increased burden on the local casualty department rather than the local crematorium. If only he had a few assassins like Scarlatti instead of a bunch of amateurs, the Triads would once more command the fear that was their due.

Dawn broke over Beachy Head. On the shoreline below the cliffs, waves crashed with a wild thunderous roar, swirling and spraying their white foam skywards. Three white vans came to a halt on the cliff top and their passengers disembarked. This was to be no car-boot sale.

Master Lau stood quite still, gazing out to sea, as though in a trance, for a long while, then turned back to give his instructions.

Two of the assassins unloaded their human cargo from the back of the second van, a battered and dishevelled-looking Goldman and a heavily sedated Murphy.

All of Lau's men were meticulously dressed in black with matching ornamental swords like some bizarre nocturnal away strip.

Hymie was beginning to wish he'd become an electrician. Had he stuck to his apprenticeship, he would probably be rich and contented by now, with a fat wife and 2.2 children, instead of staring down the barrel of a .45 handgun. Still, who needed it? This was *real*, more was the pity!

The ground cover on top of the cliff wasn't best suited to hiding spectators, even those as lithe and slender as Steffie Scarlatti. She had camouflaged herself and taken refuge behind one of those wind-blasted trees that seem to lean at an angle of forty-five degrees to the horizon for years with no ill effect, other than falling into the sea when the soil erosion catches up with it.

Goldman's car, the ill-fated Zebaguchi 650, lay concealed beneath two tonnes of camouflage. It had proved nigh on impossible to make the blasted thing blend in with the landscape so she had gone for the Iron Age burial-mound look. It was nothing more than a piece of scrap iron anyway.

"Why should Lau have all the fun?" she thought, as she shouldered her newly acquired anti-tank gun, flicked up the sights at the end of the barrel and took a final look at her make-up in the rear-view mirror. It was party time! She lined up the third of the white vans in her sights and teased the trigger with her fingertip.

Lau had a distinct and persistent feeling of unease. He hadn't left a soufflé in the oven. Neither had he lived to be sixty-three without having a talent for survival. He'd sent out his scouts before arriving on the cliff top, but as yet had received no reported sightings of Ms Scarlatti, or of anything suspicious. Yet he trusted his instincts…she would be there.

"Well, gentlemen, any last requests? A cigarette perhaps? Some new office furniture, Mr Goldman?" Levity somehow didn't suit Lau, he was too pompous.

"How about some prawn balls with P Lau rice?" quipped Hymie, who felt somehow liberated by having nothing left to lose but his life.

Lau scowled. He was on the point of signalling for the headsman when he checked himself and an evil leer spread across his normally inscrutable face.

"What do you hope to gain from this, Wun Hung Lo?" snapped Hymie in a final flash of defiance.

"You are simply the bait, gentlemen, for the diva of death."

"You want Steffanie Scarlatti? Is that it? I can tell you where she lives."

"I fear it is too late, Mr Goldman."

His prophetic words died on his lips as, looking up, he finally caught sight of a glint of light in the tree cover on the horizon.

VAVAVOOOOMMM!!!!

Lau stood pointing at the trees with his mouth open, but all anyone could hear was the roar of a high-speed projectile as it blasted across the sky, locked on its target. The third van of the trio burst into flames, its petrol tank exploded, sending black smoke up into the ozone layer. Within a few minutes all that remained of Ford's finest was a charred remnant.

"Try selling that on ebay!" snarled Scarlatti.

Hymie gazed across the cliff top. Funny, he didn't recall seeing a burial mound there before. Well, it was burning away nicely now.

"It's that ruddy woman again, let's get outta here fast, Mike!"

Lau focused his binoculars on what looked like a dancing shrub. Scarlatti was desperately hopping around trying to avoid the flames created by the blowback from the AT gun. Their eyes met across the field of battle.

She discarded the cumbersome metal pipe and unstrapped her beloved handgun, a modified Colt 1911, from its holster. "Come and get it while it's *hot*, boys!" she shouted above the noise of the holocaust.

The Lau pro-celebrity synchronised hit team was nothing if not ambitious. From all directions they broke cover and ran at the crazy bitch. Unfortunately for them she had a weapon and knew how to use it.

Gunfire rang out across the land.

BLAM, BLAM-BLAM, BLAM-BLAM, BLAM, BLAM-BLAM-BLAM-BLAM!!

The cliff top was beginning to resemble Boot Hill.

Whoever said "he who lives by the sword shall die by the sword" has been dead for many years. He was killed by a runaway horse. No one uses swords these days except as ornamental letter-openers, apart from psychotic Triad hit men with a hankering for the glory days of the samurai. So it will surely come as no surprise that the outcome of the first innings was Swords nil, Guns and Rockets eight. There was no second innings.

It was while Mike and Hymie were contemplating how

irksome it could be lying facedown in a pile of rabbit droppings that the Seventh Cavalry rode over the hill in the shape of DI Decca and a police armed response unit. The cavalcade of cop cars paraded out along the cliff top and police marksmen were deployed to cover their entrance onto the field of battle. The area was duly cordoned off and most of the survivors apprehended for questioning. Master Lau, however, was not among those detained.

As the sun climbed over the wreckage of his Zebaguchi 650, Hymie gazed forlornly into the middle-distance, tears of regret welling in his eyes. He approached the colossal wreck with an aching void in his heart. It was foolish to love a car, and yet, why not? In this veil of tears called life, what made *more* sense – to put one's trust in man, with all his fickleness and deceit, or in a machine that gave long and lasting service? He stood and surveyed the ruins of his car with a feeling of total desolation. What was left for him now?

"Don't get too close, Goldman! It's only a *car*," shouted Decca.

"*Only a car*?! Do you understand nothing, you crass commercial oaf?! It was the last of its kind. The last Zebaguchi 650 anywhere in the country. What would *you* know anyway, you…you *Mondeo driver!*"

Sometimes there were just no words.

"That's enough bull for one day, Goldman. You're under arrest for causing an affray." Decca smiled. Some days you couldn't help liking this job.

Part Eighteen

"I don't know. How many times do I have to tell you?" pleaded Hymie.

"As many as it takes, Goldman."

He was in a police cell late at night.

"Oof! Uurgh! Aaargh!"

He was spitting out blood and teeth, but Terse continued

to hit him. This couldn't be *right*, this couldn't be happening, it was an outrage.

"You can't do this! This is England, we have the rule of law, we have rights."

"If everyone has rights then no one does!" cried Terse, and then punched him to the ground again.

"You did it, didn't you? You're *scum*. I know your sort and you did it all right."

Hymie's mouth opened in an involuntary shriek, seeming to last forever. He was looking through the eyes of Eddie Munch, down on the Oslo fjord sinking into an apocalyptic orange sky, feeling all the existential angst of his race. This *couldn't* be real, he was from Finchley.

He woke up, sweat pouring down his face.

"What the hell am I mixed up in?" thought Hymie. "It's getting so bad that I can't sleep without class B drugs and class A nightmares."

He was back at 792A Finchley Road, lying on the floor. He sat up and lit a cigarette. He hated himself for his weaknesses but they were a part of him; he might just as well have loathed himself for breathing. Even his solicitor had been surprised when they let him out on bail. Benny had advanced him the bail money against the insurance proceeds from the Zebaguchi 650, though he wasn't entirely sure he had paid the premiums, or even that it was registered in his name. Possession was nine tenths of the law.

Finally, as the icing on the cake, he had persuaded the judge to let him pay off his parking fines at the heady rate of £2 a week. Judges didn't live in the real world, so Mr Justice Williamson probably thought he was driving a hard bargain!

Mike had been released with a caution; not to associate with Hymie Goldman, and been bound over to keep the peace for twelve months.

Hymie picked up the newspaper he had been using as a blanket and re-read the lead story. Under the headline "Beachy Head horror!" it gave a somewhat skewed account of events, focusing on the stunningly attractive chief suspect, Steffanie Scarlatti.

There were pictures of her in a state of semi-undress looking like Miss Whiplash in a black Basque with what could have been a black riding crop. They *had* to be fakes – the photos that is.

It wasn't that she didn't have the figure for it, just that she didn't seem to care enough about the money to let them take the snaps. As usual he was wrong; money was always in fashion with La Scarlatti, so much so that she had sold topless photos of herself to numerous top-shelf publications while the cult of her celebrity still burned bright. Now languishing in Holloway Prison awaiting the full-blown trial, Steffie Scarlatti had become something of a media celeb already.

Master Lau was a name no one was mentioning. Hymie was firmly of the belief that this was because no one had ever heard of him. He may have been a bit of a tit but he didn't have a photogenic cleavage.

Sergeant Terse had been transferred to traffic duties after the Beachy Head horror. The view from the top was that the casualties would have been significantly lower without his involvement and that a spell in traffic would calm him down. This at least was the view *before* Monday 23rd August or "Black Monday" as it was afterwards known in traffic circles.

The day commenced as dismally as most Monday mornings, with hordes of Vectra-bound reps and MPV-mums on school runs tooting and fist-waving at each other in the age-old ritual of the rush-hour traffic jam. Fate, however, was about to play a hand in events.

At 08:00, Sergeant Terse and PC Reidy were proceeding along the Broadway, Hendon, in a westerly direction. At 08:06 their attention was caught by the "Plink! Plink!!" sound of an expensive computerised traffic-signalling system going for a Burton.

Sergeant Terse turned to his junior colleague and said, "Oh, dearie me, Reidy, we had better conduct the traffic until such time as the engineers can be called for." To which PC Reidy replied, "Yes, Sarge. I'll go and call for assistance at once."

With the general air of a master conductor assuming charge of a forty-piece orchestra, Terse strode out into the path of the oncoming vehicles, narrowly avoiding death or serious injury. He raised the baton in his right hand and miraculously the traffic all around him stood still. He smirked.

At this point he appeared drastically to overestimate his own skills and started waving the baton around with wild and enthusiastic abandon, as though about to launch into a high-speed rendition of the *William Tell* overture. The traffic moved forwards in all directions simultaneously and pandemonium ensued – screeching brakes, colliding cars and everywhere the sound of breaking glass, metal and plastic.

BANG! CRUNCH!! TINKLE TINKLE!!! KERRRUNCH!!!!

Row upon row of assorted vehicles now cluttered up the street in all directions, like some giant discarded metal concertina. At this point Terse became more introspective.

"Oi, PC Plod!" cried a distressed motorist.

"*Sergeant*, thank you!"

"Sorry… . Oi, *Sergeant* Plod! What are you going to do about my ruddy car? It's completely knackered!"

"Get that pile of junk out of here, lady, before I arrest you for obstructing the highway!"

He looked around for signs of Reidy and reinforcements, but finding none quickly removed his helmet and started to walk off down the street.

"Oi, pig, where do you think you're going?" asked a passing yobbo.

Sergeant Terse was about to claim to be going off duty when he caught sight of the huge biker blocking his path and thought better of it.

"You're nicked, Scumball!" he said, forcefully.

The Dudley Road chapter of the Walsall Sixty-Niners had spent weeks cleaning and polishing the chrome on their choppers and tuning their engines to the peak of perfection. They had planned to spend a jolly weekend of mayhem and carnage in Brighton before returning home after tea on Sunday. Being stuck in a pile-up in Hendon had never been part of their plans and their feelings towards the man responsible bordered on the homicidal. Terse neither knew, nor cared.

Mitch Maguire, their leader, weighed in at twenty-two stones in his stockinged feet, not that he ever wore stockings; there was nothing funny about *him*. At six feet six inches he towered over Terse and stood glowering at the poor specimen of a policeman before him as though disappointed that his country had come so low. He needn't have worried.

Terse pulled back his right fist and straightway plunged it into the man mountain's massive gut. He doubled up, as much with surprise at the other's temerity as with pain, then recovered and landed a blow on Terse's left ear. They traded punches for a few minutes until the sergeant realised that without back-up he was on a hiding to nothing, and the biker realised that spending the rest of the week in a police cell wouldn't go down too well with the missus.

Maguire climbed back onto his chopper and started to rev up the engine.

VVVVRRRoooommmm, vvrrooom!!

Terse caught sight of PC Reidy ambling along the pavement in his general direction, whistling a happy tune. He hoped that meant that help was on its way, otherwise it was just him and Reidy, and Reidy was about as much use as a fart in a spacesuit.

Terse presented his open palm to the approaching biker.

"Come off it, fatso, even you couldn't be *that* daft. You so much as scuff my shoes and you'll be on the wrong end of a charge sheet as long as your arm."

Maguire's face displayed a complete lack of concern as he revved up his bike once more, before finally releasing the handbrake. The chopper lunged forward menacingly, threatening to flatten Terse where he stood, but the bloody-minded copper maintained his absurd composure. Like some bizarre suburban matador he spun on his right heel, lurching out of the path of the chromium-plated killing machine.

Terse looked on with an air of smug satisfaction as the hairy biker flew hell-for-leather through his vacated airspace, maintained his trajectory with sylph-like grace for several seconds and then ploughed headlong into an approaching articulator.

The crunch of breaking bones and mangled motorbike parts could be heard streets away.

"Call an ambulance, Reidy!"

Reidy arrived at his destination just in time to see the dénouement and as instructed promptly radioed for medical assistance.

"They'll never get through the traffic, Reidy, we'd better *carry* him to the hospital!"

"You're never going to move him in that state, Sarge?"

"No, but he doesn't know that, Reidy," he said, with a sardonic smile.

It was at this juncture that the rest of the Sixty-Niners decided that they would never live it down if they sat idly by and let a copper get the better of their leader.

"Oi, pig! Like to try that again with the six of us?"

They dismounted and the six leather-clad nutters marched as one towards Terse, swinging their ugly-looking bike chains about like heavy metal jewellery.

"We're gonna re-arrange your face, Scumball!"

This was something Terse could understand. The Road Traffic Acts failed to grab his attention. The Highway Code was apt to pall over the long haul, but give him a bunch of plug-uglies with chains and he was on home ground. He unfastened his truncheon.

"Boys, boys, give me a break."

"Where do you want it, pig? Arm, leg or head?"

"I've got my quota of dumb-ass thugs for this month. Do you really want to join Giant Haystacks over there on C ward? Just put down the necklaces while you can still walk!"

It was pure chance that Inspector Ray Decca should be on duty and passing down the Broadway at the time all this was going down. Certainly he had little chance of avoiding being re-united with his former sergeant.

Once he knew why he had been sitting in his car for the past hour, while a sergeant in the traffic division had a punch-up with a gang of bikers, he reflected that it could only really have been Barry Terse; the man had an innate gift for violent contretemps.

Terse *belonged* in homicide; whether as a statistic or a detective he wasn't entirely sure, but the truth would out.

"Hold it there, gents!" said DI Decca.

It was difficult to say who was the more surprised: Terse, at the sudden re-appearance of his former boss, or the bikers at being referred to as "gents".

"Keep your nose out, Goldilocks, or we'll re-arrange your face too!" said the most eloquent of the Neanderthals to Decca.

"It's okay, Chief, everything's under control," said Barry Terse.

"That's *one* way of looking at it, Sergeant."

"I've called for backup, sir."

"Thanks, Reidy," said Decca.

The penny dropped with the bikers. "Hey! Goldilocks is a pig too!"

Their difficulty seemed to be in knowing which policeman to hit first. Terse was in his element; stylishly unwinding a bike chain from around his neck with his left hand while executing a perfect polo swing with his truncheon hand.

"OOOF!"

One of the six lay indisposed on the pavement, holding his leather-clad genitals in obvious agony.

"Enough! Put the chains down now!" cried Decca. He was holding a revolver in his outstretched hand. He aimed it at the chest of the nearest biker.

The biker stood very still and appeared to be struggling with deep emotions.

"'Ere, Chief, you can't go pulling guns on people. Low-life scum they may be, but this isn't the answer, believe me," declared Terse.

"Thank you for those words of support, Sergeant. Now, read these men their rights and cuff them to the car."

Never known to disobey a direct order, Terse and Reidy soon had the bikers handcuffed at all points around the inspector's car. Only when this pressing task had been completed did Terse return to his recent grievance.

"I'm sorry to have to do this, Chief, but you're under arrest for the unlawful use of a firearm."

Inspector Decca's face assumed a look of total bemusement.

"And they told me you didn't have a sense of humour, Terse!"

"This isn't a laughing matter, sir."

"Sergeant, do you realise the seriousness of your allegation? Do you really want this on your record?"

Reidy was looking at the ground and shuffling his feet; clearly wishing he could be elsewhere. The bikers and other onlookers were beginning to warm to Sergeant Terse.

"The rulebook is my bible, sir, and you're in clear breach of Section 4.2 of the Firearms Code."

"That'll do, Sergeant. Here…this was the weapon in question; it's a kid's toy gun. A replica made in Taiwan. I had occasion to take it off a juvenile delinquent earlier this morning."

"'Ere, have you been drinking, Chief?"

"What's that got to do with anything? So, I had a drink a few hours ago, it was old Jack Harrison's leaving do. Do you think I'd be *that* stupid?" Secretly the doubts were beginning to creep in.

"I'm afraid I'll have to ask you to blow into the bag, Chief. We can't have Joe Public thinking we think we're above the law, now can we? The job's flippin' hard enough as it is."

One blow in a bag later and Inspector Ray Decca was looking distinctly embarrassed.

"Look, Sergeant…Barry, it could happen to anyone. I need hardly tell you as a highly esteemed colleague, Barry, er…"

"That's not what you thought when you had me transferred to traffic, Chief."

"A misunderstanding, Barry, old son, nothing more. Stick with me and you'll be an inspector before you know it."

"What, in *traffic*?"

"Of course not, me old mate. I knew it the moment I saw

you handle those bikers. You belong in homicide, Terse. I'm only sorry I didn't recognise the fact sooner."

"So am I, Chief. You're nicked for being drunk in charge of a motor vehicle."

"But Sergeant...look, I barely turned the crystals pink. By the time we get down to the station for a blood test I'll be in the clear. Besides, I'm late for my appointment at the Marriage Guidance."

"You goin' to RELATE, Chief?"

The sergeant's hard-bitten exterior became noticeably less hard-bitten.

"Do yourself a favour, Chief, get a divorce."

Decca looked at him for some elaboration, but none was forthcoming.

"Oh and if I don't get the transfer back to homicide by next week I might just have second thoughts about booking you."

Well, thought Barry Terse as he walked to the tube station, principles were one thing, but you didn't have to be stupid about them.

Part Nineteen

The RELATE offices were in a converted semi-detached house formerly occupied by the Citizens' Advice Bureau. It seemed that marriage guidance had become more of a pressing social need than advising the local population on what to do when their furniture was repossessed. Marriage itself seemed to be in terminal decline in the modern live-for-today era, when responsibility and commitment had become dirty words.

Rita O'Nions had been a counsellor with the Marriage Guidance Council for many years. She had seen and heard everything from the sublime to the ridiculous and thought she knew it all. It was true she had resuscitated a few marriages along the way, in the main by metaphorically clumping together heads that should have known better, but she was inclined to be prejudiced against men.

"Hello, Mrs Decca, do take a seat. No, not *that* one, that's mine. Is your husband with you today?"

"No, not yet. He said he had a few things to sort out at the station first."

"Oh, righty-ho. I didn't realise he worked on the railways. *He's* the one, is he, ho, ho!"

"No, the *police* station, he's a police inspector."

"Oh, ah, yes."

"He shouldn't be too long, it's just difficult getting time off when you're in the police."

"Perhaps we should start the ball rolling in his absence?"

"If you think it would help."

"Of course. Tell me, Mrs Decca, or may I call you Gladys?"

"Well, if you insist, although my name's Sheila."

"Oh, of course. I couldn't read your writing. So tell me, Sheila, what seems to be the problem with your marriage? Has your husband been violent or unfaithful?"

"No, nothing like that."

"Does he drink or take drugs?"

"No, nothing out of the ordinary."

"Well, that's an encouraging start, don't you think?"

"If you say so."

"So what's causing the trouble between you?"

"It's his job. He's hardly ever at home and when he is, it's as if I'm not there."

"I see, well nobody likes to be undervalued, but have you tried to improve things between the two of you? Do you ever have sexual relations?"

"Not with each other. Not for a long while."

"So you have sexual relations with someone else?"

"No, but I've thought about it."

"I'm sure you have. It's important to feel satisfied and sex can be a very positive force in a relationship."

"He was never what you'd call a great lover. It was all over in about five minutes."

"You poor dear. But you'd be amazed, in some circles five

minutes is regarded as a marathon. Many perfectly normal couples don't have relations as often as they used to." She looked wistfully out of the window for a moment.

"He sounds like a good provider anyway. Inspectors in the police must be reasonably well paid, I would have thought."

"Yes, but we don't live in a hunter-gatherer society anymore, do we?"

"No, no. Nevertheless, gone are the days when a husband could be relied upon to provide a decent standard of living for his family. These days they're all a bunch of sponging loafers who run off with next door's *au pair* when you're not paying attention."

"You poor thing," said Sheila Decca, "and *you* a marriage guidance counsellor too. It just shows you."

"Oh no, dear, I wasn't speaking of myself, no. Just a *friend*, you understand."

Outside in reception Ray Decca leant down to the sliding glass window and asked to see Mrs Onions.

"Don't for heaven's sake call her *that*, will you? It's *O'Nions*. She gets ever so narked. Especially recently. You'd think her husband was having it off with the *au pair* or something."

He smirked at the girl's indiscretion.

"She's in interview room two. Just go right in, she'll be expecting you."

He knocked and entered the room on hearing a muffled sound from the other side of the door.

"Sorry I'm late, there was a terrible traffic jam in Hendon."

"Please sit down, Mr Decca. Excuse us for starting without you but I'm a bit busy today so Sheila has been filling me in on the background."

"Fine," he said, resignedly.

"Good, then let's make a start. The objective is for you both to do the talking, work out what's going wrong in your marriage and agree on how you can fix it and for me to act as an impartial adviser. There are no right or wrong answers here, it's all about what works for you. Successful relationships depend upon good communications. So, Sheila, would you start by telling Ray what's going wrong from your point of view..."

"Yes, Rita. Ray knows how I feel: you can't have good communications when one person in a relationship is never there. And when he is there he ignores me. I get more attention from the postman."

"What does that mean? What has the postman got to do with anything? You know I have a difficult job, Sheila. I can't just leave at five o'clock when I'm on a case, it's just not that kind of job. When I do get home, I'm drained. I just want to relax in front of the television and forget about the day I've had. I can't make polite chit-chat about Mrs Doodah from the women's knitting circle."

"So why don't you give up the job?" asked Sheila.

"I can't. At my age what else could I do?" replied Ray.

"I don't know, but at least we'd be *together*."

"Besides, I love the job, I always have," he admitted.

Rita reflected that the incidence of divorce among marriage guidance counsellors was one of the worst of any profession. They didn't tell you that when you started.

"As you can see, Rita, there's just no romance left in our marriage. He's married to the police force, not to me," complained Sheila.

"Can't you try to meet Sheila halfway, Ray?"

"Halfway? Where do you mean? Enfield?"

"Buy her the occasional bunch of flowers, take her out for a meal."

"For heaven's sake, woman, we've been married twenty-three years. How many married couples do *you* know that even preserve the romance more than a few months after the honeymoon?"

"Sheila, I sympathise. Ray, if you want to get the best out of your marriage, you need to try to find ways of building bridges with your wife. Can't you suggest anything?"

He raised his eyes to the ceiling and stood up.

"I'm sorry, Sheila, I have to go. I've got a departmental meeting at two o'clock."

"Ray, we need to sort this out."

"I'm afraid it'll have to keep."

He crossed the room, opened the door and passed down the corridor back to the street. He could imagine what they were saying about him, but he had no choice, couldn't they see that?

Part Twenty

In her exquisitely decorated and tastefully furnished apartment in the West End, Mrs Edna Timmins was holding court. She looked like everyone's favourite grandma, the archetypal, sweet-natured, white-haired, little old lady. You could imagine her serving tea and scones at a village tea party or singing feebly in the congregation of a rural parish church.

Looks could be deceptive. In reality she was a hard-bitten multi-millionairess and ruthless bitch, running every kind of racket from drug-pushing to gun-running. She controlled all the wild-flower pressing from Golders Green to Dagenham and was just moving in on the WI's jam-making monopoly west of Croydon. She enjoyed the disparity between her public and private faces and sustained her public image by the convenient fiction of telling her gangland acquaintances that she worked for a schizoid drug dealer called Baron Chang. The picture she painted of him was so appalling that they were all delighted to deal with her, as his representative, instead.

"Queen's bishop to king's knight five. Checkmate, I believe, Lau. I win again."

"You are a remarkable player, Mrs T," said Lau, patronisingly.

He studied her wrinkled face, looking for the slightest glimmer of weakness or frailty, but found none. Her face was as blank as a saggy ceremonial mask.

From beneath his covered cage in the corner of the room, Cedric the macaw invited their guest to join him in a nut.

Lau shot up in his chair and assumed a defensive posture until he realised he was beginning to look ridiculous.

"You, on the other hand, Lau, would do well to read your Spassky," resumed the purple-rinsed one, "though I sometimes have my suspicions that you're not playing to the best of your ability."

"My dear lady, whatever gives you such an impression?"

"Anyone with your talent for saving his own skin must surely know all about chess. Although it's the game of kings, not killers."

"If I am honest, dear lady, my own interests are more in the field of TV game shows."

"You surprise me yet again, Lau. However, getting back to the pig, it's a great pity your unfailing instinct for self-preservation didn't extend to the baron's pig."

"My dear Mrs Timmins, I can assure you that the baron's interests are of paramount importance to me. Scarcely a day passes without my offering up prayers to heaven that the baron should receive his just deserts in this life and the next. If I could have retrieved the golden pig for him already, I would have done so. Unfortunately, I have my suspicions as to its whereabouts but no hard evidence."

"Have you forgotten so soon, man, that it was *I* who paid you to kill Goldman. Is it your idea of a joke to allow him to wander around freely? If so, it's in extremely poor taste. Will you finish the job or shall I tell the baron that you were unequal to the task?"

"I understand and share your frustration, Mrs T, I really do. I was on the point of disposing of him recently when the police arrived to spoil my plans. Goldman is a surprisingly resourceful man."

"Surprising is right!"

"Nevertheless, he will not last long with me on his trail," stressed Lau.

"You have a plan?"

"I am never without one, I assure you, Mrs T."

"Well, tell me then how you plan to pay the baron his £2,000,000?"

"Two million pounds? But the golden pig isn't worth as much as that, surely?"

"It's worth whatever someone is prepared to pay for it, Lau. To the baron it is worth £2,000,000."

"It is uncanny how you know his mind so well, Mrs T. You must be *very* close."

"We are. So tell me about this plan of yours."

He was about to say that he was jolly well going to if she gave him half a chance, but he fought back his irritation. The illusion of inscrutability must be preserved.

"The golden pig is in the possession of Steffanie Scarlatti, so *if* I am able to retrieve it, I will let the baron know in due course. As for raising the £2,000,000 he asks for, I have a new stratagem; a betting scam..."

"What, rigging a few races?"

"Not just any races, dear lady...*the* race; the Cheltenham Gold Cup. I know of your sporting interests and thought it would appeal to your sense of occasion. I have a number of contacts in the leading stables around the country and plan to call in a few favours."

"And you are confident of success, Lau?"

"I can be very persuasive."

"And this will bring me, I mean the baron, £2,000,000?"

"At a conservative estimate. Of course, I should need a small contribution to defray expenses. Shall we say £30,000, dear lady?"

"*Dear* is right, Lau. Given more details of what you plan to do with the money and some security I may be able to raise £20,000, but I am not independently wealthy and it would be out of the question to ask the baron for the money in the circumstances."

"So be it, madam."

"And Goldman?"

"That, if I may say so, is the beauty of my scheme. The favourite this year is a horse called..."

"Summer Lightning."

"Precisely. What could be better than fabricating a kidnapping plot and persuading the owner to employ

Goldman as bodyguard to the horse? My confederates would then have an open field to dope the animal."

"And Goldman?"

"As you wish...we can either kill him or so discredit his pathetic little business that no one would hire him to protect so much as a child's bag of sweets."

"Or both."

"Exactly, dear lady."

"I like it, Lau, I like it. But make no mistake. This is your last chance. The baron doesn't suffer fools gladly."

"Who does, Mrs T, who does? I will call you to confirm the arrangements in the usual way."

The sound of a bird's wings flapping was heard outside. She turned to see what it was and when she turned back he was gone and all that remained was a cloud of blue smoke.

Did he *really* imagine he could impress her with his Ali Bongo magic tricks?

Part Twenty-One

The telephone trilled intrusively like a budgie on heat. Otherwise all was quiet, if anywhere in North London could be said to be quiet.

The intrepid Goldman lumbered across his empty office and snatched up the receiver. He didn't want to be Hymie Goldman anymore – it just meant trouble.

"Spear and Jackman!" he yelled into the mouthpiece.

"Sorry, I thought this was the number for JP Confidential."

"It is, lady, but we have to be careful," said Hymie, more calmly.

"Do you? Why?"

"No names, no pack drill, I'm sure you understand. What can we do for you?"

She sounded well-to-do, if you *could* sound affluent, well educated and stylish on the phone.

"I gather you have experience with horses, Mr Goldman."

He resisted the urge to say "nothing was ever proven" and started trawling through what passed for his mind to see if he either knew anything about horses or about anyone who may be interested in them. He drew a blank.

"Yes, I adore them," said Hymie, unfazed.

"Oh, splendid. My name is Hunting-Baddeley, Lucinda Hunting-Baddeley, of the Suffolk Hunting-Baddeleys. You were recommended to me by an old friend of the family as a good man to have around in a tight spot."

How did she know? He'd been in a tight spot for years.

"Of course, but could you be a little more specific?"

"I thought I was being as clear as crystal; I want you to come over and babysit Summer Lightning in the run-up to Chelters, as we've had kidnapping threats."

"Chelters?" he queried.

"The Gold Cup."

"Oh yes, of course."

She wasn't on acid, she was just la-di-da.

"Well, perhaps I can drop in and see you to agree terms?" she suggested.

"Spiffing. Or should I come to see you? It's no trouble," he added hastily.

"Thank you, but I'm often down in the old metrop, so it's no bother and I rather like to see who I'm dealing with on their home turf. I always think you can tell a great deal about someone by their taste in furnishings."

He wanted to laugh hysterically. She wouldn't be able to tell much about him from *his* furnishings; he didn't have any. What did that signify except bankruptcy?

"Did you say who recommended me? I'd like to thank them personally."

"Why, it was Edna Timmins, such a nice little old lady and so knowledgeable about equestrian matters. She did ask me not to mention her by name, but I couldn't see what harm it could do. Of course you'd want to know you had a satisfied client, but do keep it to yourself, please, as I wouldn't want to upset the old dear."

"Mrs Timmins? Was the world going mad? Why would *she* be recommending *him*?" Something didn't add up.

"Of course, Mrs Hunting Badly."

"Hunting-Baddeley."

"Quite so."

"So shall we say next Tuesday afternoon at three p.m.? You're at 792A Finchley Road, I believe."

He groaned inwardly. "Yes. Yes, of course. I look forward to it." He replaced the receiver.

It was inconceivable that Mrs Timmins should have recommended him. The last time they had spoken she had threatened him with bodily injury, and she had meant it. Perhaps she had something against this Hunting-Baddeley woman and thought she was doing her a bad turn. Perhaps she disliked horses and thought he would make a hash of the job. It didn't really matter; he didn't intend to ask her and there was no other way he could find out. He still seemed to have come out on top…as long as he could acquire some office furniture by Tuesday.

He lifted the receiver again and dialled Murphy's number. He hadn't seen Mike since just after their last police interrogation, but felt sure he must be missing him. The phone number was unobtainable.

As he sat there wondering how on earth he could contact his old pal without going over to his dismal flat, the clumping of heavy boots on the stair outside heralded the arrival of the man mountain himself. He wasn't looking any too chipper.

"You may not believe it, but I've just been trying to phone you. Your phone's been disconnected. Anything I can do?" asked Hymie, solicitously.

"I think you've done enough already, you great spawny-eyed wassock! A few weeks ago I was an honest, hardworking doorman with a secure job. Now look at me!"

Tact and the desire not to have his face re-arranged kept the irrepressible one's mouth tightly buttoned, but he couldn't help noticing what a state his old friend was in; he hadn't shaved, his clothes were badly creased and his shoelaces were undone.

"I can't get a job as a bouncer *anywhere*. I've lost my flat and I feel like I'm constantly being watched."

"Try not to be so paranoid, Mike," said Hymie, himself a prince among paranoiacs.

"I'm trying, but it's not so easy when everyone's out to get you!" lamented Mike.

"Don't worry, be happy," sang Hymie, tunelessly. "I have a new case, Mike, and I want *you* to be in on it with me. We'll be laughing all the way to the bank, believe me, it's money for old rope…"

"Do me a favour, H…"

"Sure."

"*Don't* do me any more favours! Or I might just forget we go way back and beat nine kinds of crap out of you!"

Hymie hadn't realised there *were* nine kinds of crap but could see this wasn't a good time to broach the subject.

"Mike, all we have to do is baby-sit one measly racehorse."

"Oh, pardon me, I was forgetting you're a qualified vet, known throughout North London as the *horseman of Finchley*…what could be simpler?"

"Come on, Mike, what can it take to look after a racehorse? We just have to make sure no one nicks it before the Gold Cup."

"Where's the catch?" asked Mike, like a man covered in bee stings being asked to collect some honey.

"I don't know what you mean."

"If this is one of *your* cases, there *must* be a catch somewhere, it stands to reason."

"Well, I wouldn't put it quite like that, but we do have to find some office furniture for a meeting with the client next Tuesday. But other than that…"

"Other than that? Where are you going to find some office furniture that quick?"

"I thought maybe you had some contacts," said Hymie, hopefully.

"You thought wrong. I'm broke and my credit rating is only just on the right side of criminal. A blind beggar wouldn't lend me a brass farthing to please his dying mother. Don't look at me like that either; it's not my fault."

"Look, Mike, this could be our best chance ever of making some easy money. Trust me. We're not gonna throw it all away just because we can't get our hands on a few sticks of furniture, surely?"

"Why do I know I'm gonna live to regret this?"

"You *do* know someone then?"

"Hold it, no promises, Hymie, but I think that perhaps, maybe, possibly I might know someone who could help."

"Great!"

"Wait a minute, what's in it for me?"

"The satisfaction of a job well done?"

"How much?"

"You get me the furniture and I'll cut you in for a third of whatever I make."

"A half!"

"Forty per cent?"

"A half!"

"You're a hard man to do business with," protested Hymie.

"Do we have a deal?" persisted Mike.

"All right…half it is," agreed Hymie. What was there to lose? Half of nothing was still nothing.

"Oh, and there's one other thing," added Mike.

"What's that?"

"You couldn't lend me a fiver for breakfast could you, I'm starving?"

Hymie reached into his shirt pocket and retrieved one of the chronically few surviving specimens from Lucy Scarlatti's thousand-pound advance. In trying to advertise his own commercial acumen to a would-be business partner he could hardly admit he couldn't spare a fiver.

Mike headed off to the Black Kat to refuel, leaving Hymie to mull over how they were going to raise enough capital to get the horse baby-sitting business off the drawing board.

He discounted Ceefer Capital. Somehow he expected them to try and tie him up in watertight legal agreements, even if they were willing to cough up. Besides, he was saving them for a rainy day. Since every day was a rainy day at JP Confidential, he probably meant a torrential downpour.

"I'm about due for another pop at the bank that likes to say yes," he thought. "Surely they will take the long view and realise that by supporting my fledgling business now, they will reap the benefits tomorrow." It was an interesting theory.

He thought of his bank manager, Tony someone or other (Turbot, wasn't it?) and his confidence in the scheme began to deflate, like a dinghy with a slow puncture. Turbot was your archetypal modern bank manager; lacking in imagination, emasculated to the point of needing a chit from head office to wipe his nose, and having an absurd obsession with collateral. He reflected on the gross unfairness of life; on how this two-dimensional clod should command public respect, while he, a hard-working professional man, should be censured and derided – and then he wrote a letter, never intending to send it.

Dear Mr Turbot [no] Dear Tony [yes, that sounds better],

Thank you for your letter of the 14th inst [whatever an "inst" is], explaining why you had charged me fifty-seven pounds and eighty-three pence in administration fees; presumably to write those charming letters telling me I was overdrawn. Nice though it was to receive them, I already knew, thank you. In fact I was sitting in my office wondering how the heck I was going to pay your original charges when the letters rolled in to notify me I had struck the bank charges' mother lode.

I am sorry to have to tell you that sarcasm is wasted on you, that you are an excrescence, not to mention a carbuncle on the bloated rear end of capitalism. Call yourself a bank manager? Why, you couldn't manage your way out of a paper bag. As for *nurturing new business*, as your advertisement claims, you wouldn't recognise an up-and-coming business if it ran over you in a bus.

Long may you rot, kind regards,
H Goldman (Mr)

He wondered if he hadn't been a little gratuitous in his insults, if fulsome in his praise early on. Nevertheless, he did feel much better for venting his spleen and went through the process of enveloping and addressing the letter just to get some kind of closure. He had done it before, but never posted them – it was just a kind of therapy.

Next he wrote the letter he was intending to send; the one that explained he needed some office furniture to clinch a lucrative contract with a well-heeled lady from Suffolk. He was sure that this was just the sort of thing the bank would like to hear.

Later that day, when a kindly old lady found a dog-eared brown envelope in the Finchley Road, she attached a dog-eared old stamp and posted it. She returned home with the sense of contentment that comes from having done a good deed in a selfish world.

Part Twenty-Two

The night was dark, pitch black with not a star in sight. A chill wind blew in from the east and anyone who had a home to go to was in it.

In the small wooden hut at the back of Pinner Parish Church strange things were beginning to happen. Arcane things, things honest respectable men and women would do well to avoid.

A tall man in a Crombie overcoat passed through the bushes alongside the hut and disappeared into its dark interior.

"Pungghhh! Puuuunnnnghhhhh!!"

The unholy congregation of the Brothers of Pung sat around in a circle, cross-legged on the floor. Their garish robes and puerile addiction to saying "pung" at the slightest provocation marked them out both as complete idiots and as dedicated members of the order. They "punged" reverently in the age-old ritual of summoning the Mighty Jong. Brother Decca hastily joined the circle with seconds to spare before the latter made his grand entrance from behind the black moth-eaten stage curtains at the back of the hall.

Only two of the brethren knew the true identity of the Mighty Jong, and they were sworn to secrecy on pain of the ritual of the boot. All members feared this dark ritual, as well they might.

It was widely believed that the MJ, as he was often referred to, was a senior ranking police officer, or why else would the rest of them be there?

The MJ stood before them in his blue-grey pinstriped suit, covered with bits of garden cane, symbolic of holy bamboo. His face was hidden behind an enormous mask; the ancient helm of Hendon, which bore a startling resemblance to an outsized policeman's helmet with two eyeholes cut out.

He assumed his place of honour at the plinth in the centre of the gathering and commenced the meeting with the usual announcements.

"Are all the tiles of our holy order safely gathered in?"

"Yes, oh Mighty Jong!"

"Are the four winds assembled in the eaves?" he continued.

"We are, oh Mighty Jong!" The words were accompanied by a ceremonial breaking of wind.

These were the lookouts posted at the four corners of the hut.

"Good, then I'll begin. Join with me in our oath of allegiance."

> By the helm of Hendon,
> By the truncheon and toecap,
> By the sword of justice,
> And the might of the right,
> We will strive 'gainst the heathen,
> 'Gainst the spirits of evil,
> Till our armies have conquered
> The things of the night.

"Punggghhh!"
"Is the first bamboo tile present?"
"Yes, oh Mighty Jong!"
"Louder, the Mighty Jong can't hear you," he cried, like a refugee from a pantomime.
"YES! Oh Mighty Jong!"
"You don't have to shout, I'm not deaf. Pray read from the *Register of Righteousness!*"
"Brethren, let us salute Brother Decca. He has excelled in the pursuit of our craft."
"Punggghhh!"
"He shall be awarded the Order of the Green Dragon, second class, in recognition of his achievements in the pursuit of the one true craft."
"Punggghhh!"
"God, this is tedious," thought Inspector Ray Decca. He'd much rather be down the pub or at the pictures...or curled up at home with a good murder mystery. Unfortunately, once you'd joined, you were stuck with it; your career would go into a terminal nosedive if you left. He had become the prisoner of his own ambition.

At the conclusion of the ceremonies they stuck what looked like a *Blue Peter* badge on him, passed around the holy scotch and soda and got totally plastered. The MJ's private minibus took them all home at midnight.

Part Twenty-Three

Mike had drawn a blank on the office furniture. It didn't help that they couldn't raise even the meagre few quid it would have taken to hire the stuff. Perhaps the aura of doom was hanging over JP Confidential and people could smell their desperation. No one was seemingly willing to throw good money after bad any longer.

"Mike, you know as well as I do that we've *got* to get hold of that office furniture and maybe a few horsy prints..."

"You mean pictures?"

"What else would I mean? By *tomorrow*, or we can kiss the job goodbye. Isn't there anyone else we can try?"

"It's a long shot, H, a real long shot, but maybe, just maybe Artful Arnie could lend us some for a few hours."

"Why do they call him Artful?"

"I dunno," said Mike.

"Well, is he reliable?"

"Yeah, you can rely on him to rip you off, but you're no slouch in that department yourself, and besides, beggars can't be choosers."

"Right. You pull this one off, Mike, and I'll make you a full partner in JP Confidential."

Mike smiled. "Isn't that a bit like making me captain on the *Titanic*, just before her maiden voyage?"

Hymie decided to feign deaf. Dead would have been better.

"Let's find this guy Arnie then, there's no time to lose."

Arnold Shoebridge, aka Artful Arnie, was a con merchant with more fingers in more pies than Little Jack Horner. People only dealt with him if they were desperate or stupid. Being both it was inevitable that Hymie Goldman should go to him for his office furniture.

After a few false leads from men in pubs they finally tracked him down to a mobile hovel on the outskirts of Elstree. He seemed to be living the life of a nomad, perched on the edge of civilisation. For the last half-mile they just followed their noses as the stench of his impromptu sanitary arrangements wafted down the lane. The place had all the ambience of a Brazilian shantytown.

Arnie was obviously distrustful of his fellow-men, as he kept two lurchers tethered on long chains outside his caravan. Their barking drew him from his pit, brandishing a double-barrelled shotgun.

"Sling yer 'ook or I shoot," shouted the debonair furniture salesman.

"You can't half pick 'em," muttered Hymie to Mike.

"Arnie! It's me, Mike Murphy. I've come about some furniture."

"Buying or selling?" asked Arnie, suspiciously.
"More of a short-term rental," said Hymie.
"Well, you'd better come in."
"The situation is this," said Mike.

Dusk was descending by the time they found themselves on home turf. They had a deal on some furniture and a great weight had thus been lifted from Hymie's mind, though Mike remained reticent about the terms of his agreement with Arnie.

Benny's Unbeatable Bakery had miraculously been restored to its former glory, though the same could not be said of its proprietor. Benny had spent weeks convalescing, first in Edgware General, and later, when he had been discharged to make room for an urgent in-growing toenail case, in a private rest home. He still had no comprehension of who or where he was and was convinced he was being pursued by leprechauns – but boredom had driven him back to work.

Mike and Hymie entered the restaurant.

"Hi Ben, good to see you on your feet again," said Hymie, brightly.

"Thanks. A waitress will be with you shortly," said his old friend, with no flicker of recognition.

"Ben, it's *me*. Hymie."

"I'm sorry, do I know you?"

"Of course, we've been friends for years – Hymie Goldman. Don't you know me, Ben?"

"Sorry, no. You're not working for the Little People are you? They're always around, watching me."

"Who are? Are you winding me up, Benny?"

"You are, aren't you? They've sent you to spy on me."

"Have you been on the funny fags again? They used to give me a persecution complex like that too."

"Who, the Little People?"

"There's no such people, you daft berk!"

"That will do. Don't go upsetting him, he's had a tough time of it lately."

It was Susie Parker, one of the waitresses.

"Oh, pardon me for breathing."

"If I must," she sighed.

"Look, I only came to see how he was," explained Hymie. "I wasn't looking for trouble."

"You never are. Trouble always seems to find you and stick with you. Benny needs complete rest, not World War Three."

"Okay, we'll go. Tell him we were asking after him."

"Cunning, you see, the Little People," continued Benny. "Never underestimate them; they have eyes and ears everywhere..."

"Ugly little devils then, eh?" said Mike.

"...but I'll outsmart them yet. I'm gonna sell up and move to Australia with Susie."

She smiled.

"Ben, you can't be serious?" Hymie sounded anxious.

She frowned.

"You stand alone. No one makes pizzas like you do, Benny."

Now it was Hymie's turn to be disconsolate. The room seemed to be doing a shimmy as his world rocked on its very foundations.

"I promised my brother Syd I'd go and visit him in Australia. It's a land of opportunity, you know."

"Benny, you haven't got a brother Syd."

"Well, who else would I go to Australia to visit?"

It seemed impossible to get through to him. Susie may have won the first round, but Hymie wasn't about to lose Benny, or his remarkable pizza, without a fight.

Part Twenty-Four

The sight of the ancient oriental Mr Fixit, Lau, sitting in front of her at visiting time in a blue pinstriped suit and with a grey, greasy pigtail hanging down his neck came as something of a surprise to Steffanie Scarlatti. Was there to be no peace, even in prison? Certainly not, but then what had *she* done to deserve peace?

"Have you come to gloat, Lau?"

"Gloat? No, my dear. I simply wondered how you were finding it in here and whether you would be interested in a small business proposition?"

"Are you in your right mind? Why would you trust *me*?"

"More so than *you* I imagine, and why trust you? I don't but I am willing to take the risk. After all, you have more to lose than I." He was the same supercilious schemer he had always been.

"You seem to forget I'm on remand at Her Majesty's pleasure and can't just walk out of here whenever it suits me," said Steffie Scarlatti.

"I can help you."

"Okay, let's suppose for the sake of argument you can, what's your price?"

"You insult me with talk of money, my dear. Has everyone become so greedy and self-seeking that they can no longer recognise an act of altruism?" he asked.

"That's rich coming from you, Lau."

"Our time is nearly up. Do you want to be free or not?"

"Free? No one is ever truly free."

"Don't go all existential on me," he complained, irritated.

"And don't you start ruddy preaching at me!" she snapped. She had momentarily forgotten where she was and raised her voice just that little too loudly.

"Quiet, Scarlatti! Visiting time is a privilege and privileges can be withdrawn." The warder was watching her closely now.

"Terrific," she thought.

Lau as ever was composed and businesslike.

"The price is removing a couple of obstacles," he said, more quietly.

"Names?"

"Timmins and Goldman."

"Hymie Goldman?" She was irritated at the thought of his still being free, while she was a prisoner.

"Precisely," confirmed Lau.

"Like taking candy from a baby," she said.

"You agree?" He couldn't see how she could refuse.

"A small enough price," remarked Steffie Scarlatti.
"Is that a yes?"
"Yes."

She would have agreed to anything. She had no scruples about lying, cheating, stealing or killing. They were means to an end, nothing more. Goldman meant nothing to her. She had enjoyed working for him as Janis Turner because he was so *laissez-faire*, but that scarcely justified any kind of loyalty.

"We will be in touch," said Lau, getting up from his chair.
"Good, I look forward to it."

The bell rang to signify the end of visiting time.

Master Lau bowed formally to his new assassin and left, presumably to return the hire suit to Moss Bros.

Part Twenty-Five

"Why me?" thought Tony Talbot, bank manager, family man and all round good bloke, if a tad tedious, as he re-read the letter on his desk. In all honesty he couldn't have told you *who* Hymie Goldman was; he was just a blip on his monthly credit risk report. Now it was *personal*. The man had gone out of his way to make his life unpleasant and he would squash him like a bug in his salad. He had never thought of himself as vindictive, mean-spirited or petty, but there was something about the tone of the letter that made him feel justified in a response that ticked any or all of the above boxes.

Where did this guy Goldman get off? It was always the bums and deadbeats who complained about bank charges. In fact it was nothing of the kind, but you couldn't get nasty with the better sort of client. He wouldn't have minded but he hadn't even had anything to do with it; there was a ruddy great computer in Peterborough that whacked out charges – they didn't leave things like that to bank managers.

He lifted the red phone on his desk. He had two phones – a green one for nice conversations and a red one for unpleasant ones. They were his own symbolic telecoms traffic light, telling him whether to stop or go. Carbuncle eh? On the bloated rear end of capitalism? What did the man *mean?* He was surely under the influence of hard liquor or drugs. Perhaps both. He would show that no-hoper Goldman, that buffoon among small businessmen. He would call in his overdraft and charge him for the letter informing him. Let him laugh that one off.

"Miss Jervis, send a letter to Mr H Goldman. I'm pulling the plug on his overdraft. Standard wording. Thank him for his letter of the 16th inst and charge him for our termination letter." His social conscience had ceased to trouble him years ago.

"Very good, Mr Talbot."

That was what he liked most about the bank – in its rigid hierarchical structure and slavish devotion to the rulebook it resembled nothing so much as the British Army.

He took his blood pressure tablets with a glass of water from the dispenser and lifted the red phone on his desk. Dialling the exclusive London premises of JP Confidential he was surprised to find the line still connected.

Hymie was in high spirits. He had a new client, some office furniture was on its way and perhaps this call was another new client in search of his unique services.

"JP Confidential, how can I help you?"

"Talbot, from the Argyll and Edinburgh Bank, Mr Goldman."

Hymie's face registered concern.

"Ah, Mr Turbot, sorry, Talbot…I'm glad you called."

"Glad, man? I've just received your letter."

"*My* letter?" Surely he couldn't have sent *that* letter.

"The one where you refer to me as 'an excrescence…a carbuncle on the bloated rear end of capitalism'," quoted Talbot, angrily.

"Are you sure it *was* from me? You see, I have a number of business rivals who would do anything to ruin my business."

"The letter is in your handwriting, man, and you've signed it."

This seemed to stump the resilient sleuth.

"Ah yes, I see. Well, apologies, Mr Talbot, I hope you realised I was only joking."

"No, I didn't, Mr Goldman. I was deeply offended by your attitude and comments."

"So, you don't think you'd be in a position to extend my overdraft just now?" asked Hymie, hesitantly.

A hollow laugh escaped the bank manager's lips. "We take our clients very seriously here at the A & E. Clearly you are dissatisfied with our service and are intending to change bankers. I was merely ringing to let you know I wouldn't stand in your way."

"Well, er…of course, it was a mistake and I wasn't planning any such thing. I'm sure we'll all have a good laugh about this in years to come."

"*You* may, Mr Goldman, but as far as I'm concerned that's out of the question. I will be sending you a written request for the repayment of your overdraft in full in today's post. Good luck with your *business*."

"But, Mr Tur…"

Click! Silence.

On the verge of bankruptcy and with no credit, how long could he last? There was only one way to find out. He was drinking once again in the last chance saloon and putting his shirt on a horse called Summer Lightning and its owner, Lucinda the hyphenated lady.

He reached for the reefer he'd been saving for just such an emergency and lit up. Now wasn't the time to re-arrange the deckchairs on the *Titanic*, it was time to switch off, tune in and check out.

A few drags later, he stood gazing out of his office window with unseeing eyes. The sun shimmered across a desert of traffic. The horizon blurred and distorted into a fusion of heat haze and morning mist. He felt like he was floating above his body, looking down on the scene of disaster with complete disinterest. What we shall laughingly refer to as his *mind* was racing through worlds as yet unknown.

Part Twenty-Six

Who can describe the terrors that lie within even a normal man's mind? The landscape of Hymie's was wild indeed; sheer cliffs of doubt descending into the slough of despond, and all encompassed by the quagmire of despair. Not an ideal holiday location, unless you fancied a change from Ibiza.

Take a trip with Hymie. Float into the void of his brain. Thoughts like far distant planets collide in the vacuous wilderness of eternity. Electric storms of fear and loathing wrack the pulse of his consciousness, tearing away the mundane, the real, the sane, leaving only the vision of a man; eight feet tall, with long white hair, a grizzled beard and holding a palmer's walking staff the size of a small tree. Wait, it *is* a small tree.

"Zeus? Odin? Buddha? Big Daddy?"

"Just call me God," said God.

"But how did I get here? Am I dead? You're not here about the parking tickets, surely?" asked Hymie.

"No. Just thought I'd drop by. You're having an hallucinogenic episode, but that doesn't make *me* any the less real. Consider yourself lucky, I don't usually make personal appearances these days. It's no fun opening supermarkets when there's one on every street corner."

"I'm glad to see you, God. Do you really know everything?"

"Yes, though most of it's not really worth knowing."

"About my life?"

"Yes, and all the others. People blame me for not taking charge of their lives for them but they should get a grip. Life's no picnic, you know."

"You're telling *me*."

"It's an opportunity...for good or ill, nothing more nor less. Those that rise to the challenge, take responsibility and don't just look out for themselves, have a rewarding and fulfilling time."

"And the rest?"

"End up shovelling the brown stuff downstairs."

"Really?"

"It's all part of the contract I signed with Satan. I get the nice people, he gets the scum; lawyers, criminals, high court judges, traffic wardens, politicians, estate agents...and so on and so forth. He's seriously overcrowded."

"Do you know what will happen next?" quizzed Hymie.

"No. Should I?"

"I don't know," said Hymie, perplexed.

"You see, you set a train of events in motion and to some extent have to wait and see what the outcome will be... nothing's predetermined. Some things are more likely than others, but anything's *possible*."

"Like me solving a big case?" asked Hymie, wistfully.

"Don't ask for *miracles*." God smiled and the room was bathed in sunlight.

"I need help, God."

"*You* need help, that's a good one! You think *you've* got problems? You don't know you're born, laddie. I have to keep records on *everyone*. It was easy when it was just Adam and Eve, but you wouldn't believe the state my admin systems are in now. Personally I blame those ruddy temps I've been using since the thirteenth century...ruddy hopeless! Most of them don't know the difference between a PC and a microwave."

Hymie just sat there gaping. It had never occurred to him that the Almighty might have problems too. When you thought about it, it made sense. Here He was, running the biggest business of all, with no one to help Him and no one even thinking He might need a hand from time to time.

Of course, God, being God, knew how to put the petty problems of even his most forlorn and forsaken sheep before his own headaches.

"Let me tell you a story, Hymie. I may call you Hymie mayn't I?"

His English grammar was a little dated, but Hymie guessed he didn't use it much. He seemed to remember it wasn't even God's native tongue.

"Sure thing, Big Guy."

"A couple of weeks ago I was sitting in my office in the Celestial Palace, or the CP as we call it, catching up on my paperwork. There was a knock at the door and a cherub poked his head around it to say there was someone at the Pearly Gates."

"He called me 'Oh Great One', which usually means they are either after something or are extracting the Michael. So I harrumphed a good deal and said couldn't the Archangel Gabriel deal with it, and they said no he ruddy well couldn't deal with it because he was out playing golf and besides, it was Lucifer himself, spoiling for a fight.

"So after a bit more umming and ah-ing and generally complaining that no one else around the place was any flaming use I flew over to QA – that's the Quarantine Area we keep for undesirables, to sort it out.

"A couple of seraphim were hovering around outside the ante-room, polishing their halos and exchanging tittle-tattle about the Devil's latest incarnation as I arrived.

"'Go on, tell me…what's he come as today, ladies?' I asked.

"'Apollo; the Greek God, not the Spacecraft. Golden curls everywhere…must have spent half the morning under a hairdryer,' they said, bitchily.

"'Well he does like to blend in on his visits here. Trying to pretend he was never really banished after all.'

"'The nerve!' they said, and I agreed with them.

"'Thank you, ladies, I suppose I'd better get this over with.'

"So I strolled into QA with my usual effusive charm, whistling the latest Lloyd Webber, 'Don't Cry For Me Somewhere or Other' I think it was, possibly Bognor Regis, and tried to get him to leave without further ado.

"'Lucie Baby! Good of you to drop by, but you know you shouldn't have.'

"'I've missed you, Big G.'

"'Thanks awfully, but you know you're not allowed in here, you old goat, it's members only.'

"'I know, but if I have to torture another ruddy lawyer I'll go mad.'

"'Fancy a beer?'

"'Sure, what have you got?' he asked.

"'Anything you can think of and a few new real ales that I'm working on.'

"'I'll have a pint of Grunge's Old Dirigible,' he said.

"The Devil clicked his fingers and a Chippendale chair appeared beneath him. Antique furniture's a passion of his when he's not tormenting lost souls.

"'Business must be bad,' I told him, trying to wind him up.

"'Are you kidding? Mankind's going down the toilet faster than I can handle. I need to rent some more space.'

"'Not from me, matey,' I assured him.

"'Look, God, I'm tired of all the recriminations and the backbiting. Tired, tired, TIRED!!!'

"'I see…you're *tired.* Ready to quit, huh, Lucie Baby? Come to throw in the towel and admit you've been wrong all along? Ready to turn over a new leaf?'

"'No.'

"'Not even just a bit?'

"'Well, maybe, but I look at it this way: we're neither of us getting any younger are we? So where's the sense in slugging it out for all eternity?' he asked.

"'What else is there? Mankind has its life, death, sex and taxes, not necessarily in that order, and we have *this*…this virtual chess game. If you're getting tired, then you can always resign. Put it another way, if you can't stand the heat, get outta the kitchen, Lucie!'

"'Not what I had in mind. Cards on the table…I've had a few setbacks I admit; that St Peter don't fight fair. But I'm big enough to take it, I don't complain.'

"'Much!'

"'If you'll just let me finish!' said Lucifer.

"'Go for it!' I said.

"'I got to thinking…'

"'A new departure for you then.'

"'…the whole thing would make a lot more sense if we settled our differences in one championship bout; my champion against your champion.'

"'The winner takes all?' I asked.

"'Exactly,' said Satan.

"'So, when I win you'll release all the tormented souls, dismantle the Kingdom of Hades and take up residence in the North Pole?'

"'Supposing there's still a polar icecap, yeah,' he said. 'And if I win?' asked the Devil.

"'In that case, as unlikely as it may be, you'll get the CP, the host of angels, the gold-plated Jacuzzi, and the fully expensed company cloud.'

"'It's a deal,' he said. 'Any rules?'

"'*You* want rules? You'd only break them anyway,' I said, antagonistically.

"'I'd pretend to be offended but I just can't be bothered today. I know *you* like rules so I thought I'd ask before you mentioned it,' said the Devil.

"'Well, rules are fine and dandy if we stick to them. What did you have in mind?'

"'Nothing...none; a championship bout to the death between two mortals,' he said.

"'A bit mediaeval, isn't it? Don't you ever move on?' I asked.

"'There's nothing to compare with a good old-fashioned punch-up.'

"'True, true. I take it we're not actually talking about a contest in the ring?'

"'No, somewhat passé. The world's their stage, their ingenuity their weapon.'"

Hymie, who had been quietly nodding off to this celestial shaggy-dog story, suddenly sat up and took notice.

"So what happened, God? Did you agree to the contest?"

"I'm afraid so, Hymie. I never could resist a challenge. It's always been a weakness of mine. They said I couldn't create the world in a week so I had to do it in six days...heck of a job that was, my back's not been the same since."

"So who are the champions...Hercules? Albert Einstein? Not Arnold Schwarzenegger?"

"That's what I wanted to talk to *you* about."

Hymie was beginning to fear the worst, but he couldn't

quite bring himself to believe that God, the omnipotent, omniscient being, could make such a dud decision.

"It's me, isn't it?" asked Hymie.

"Yes. You're my champion," said God.

"But how did that happen? I'm a complete no-hoper. Surely everyone knows that?!"

"No one's a no-hoper who believes in Me."

The white-haired giant had spun him a good yarn and he wasn't about to let him off the hook now. Hymie Goldman needed to believe in Him and so he would.

"So who do I have to fight? Hercules? Albert Einstein? Not Arnold Schwarzenegger?" He was wondering what would happen if he tried to edge out of it.

"You will know, when the time is right."

"Was I your first choice?"

"You selected yourself, Hymie. Now, I must be off. Miracles to perform and all that...you know how it is. Good luck."

He had a million unanswered questions, but Hymie never got the chance to ask one of them. A dazzling light illuminated the entire office. He covered his eyes to protect them from the searing brightness of the supreme being. Within half a nanosecond God had gone.

A voice like thunder disappearing into a long tunnel echoed after him through space. "Give up the drugs. You mustn't fail me."

The words would stay with him forever. He knew then that he had no choice, that he was irretrievably committed to this contest against some unspeakable emissary of evil and that he wasn't to be allowed even his old physiological and psychological crutch.

He sat in stunned silence for hours. The shadow patterns on the office floor swirled around him like some bizarre monochrome kaleidoscope as night passed into day, but time held no meaning for him. His mind was locked in torment. Wild imaginings overtook him and transported him to another place. He was sitting in a tram as it rattled through gaudy neon-lit streets in some distant Chinatown. From time to time he saw flashes of glass columns, chromium-plated superstructures, light displays flashing in Mexican waves across the front of mountainous tower blocks.

He flew past advertising hoardings too numerous to count, fast food restaurants, shops and bars, and everywhere were teeming, milling throngs of Chinese, like a million ants swarming through his honeycombed brain.

Another tram hove into view from the opposite direction. As it pulled alongside he noticed for the first time a girl sitting facing him. She was staring at him with her mouth open as if to speak, but her words were drowned out by the clamour of the passing throng and the clatter of the tram on its rails. In some consternation he realised that he knew her. He leant forward to speak to her, but she slumped forward into his arms and he observed with creeping horror that she had been shot. He tried to staunch the blood with his hand, but she was already dead, a lifeless thing of flesh, bleeding all over him.

He lunged at the bell and the tram lurched to a halt. People were shouting and screaming at him. Some of the passengers prodded the girl's lifeless body and recoiled in fright. All he could do was point helplessly at the retreating tram. He could have sworn he had seen a white-haired old lady moving out of sight on the lower deck. He was sure that the dart had been intended for him.

The crowd was turning nasty. He forced his way to the front of the tram and threw himself out onto the street; clear of the doors, of the menacing crowd, of his own descending panic. As he did so the driver called after him.

"You mustn't fail me! You mustn't fail me!"

When he hit the pavement he remembered where he had seen the dead girl – long ago in an apartment at 35 Riverside Drive.

Part Twenty-Seven

"Hymie! Hymie!!" Mike was gently shaking him and slapping him around the head. Since "gently" had never been in Mike's repertoire, his stocky little friend was lucky not to be adding concussion to his list of problems.

"Do this to me again, mate, and you're dead, capish? We've got a client to see in a couple of hours!"

Mike had never expected to see the day when he'd be in business with Hymie Goldman, and, now that he was, it bothered him to realise that *he* was the one taking it seriously.

"Oi, Doofus! You wanna get stoned on your time, that's up to you, but don't do it on mine!!"

Unfortunately the crumpled PI was in no fit state to heed even Mike's bellowed warning. It took a facial bath of lukewarm coffee and a good ten minutes of being frog-marched around the office before the first hesitant signs of consciousness emerged. He felt like he had been walking in slow motion down the up escalator to nowhere.

"Where am I?"

"Boy, you're sharp. Get with it, Goldman, you've got to convince this horsy dame you're an ace investigator. Some chance!"

Hymie winced.

"What day is this?"

A low groan escaped Mike's lips. "To think I gave up a good position in the dole queue for this!"

"I'm a PI, right? Do I still have any cases?" asked Hymie.

"Not if you don't pull yourself together fast. Does the name Hunting-Baddeley ring any bells?"

"Pleased to meet you, Mr Hunting-Baddeley, what can I do for you?"

"For me? Nothing. For yourself, try being a detective before I'm forced to throw you through the nearest window. Remember me? Your partner, Mike Murphy; the idiot who went into business with you against his better judgment!"

"Mike! Where's the flippin' furniture?!"

"Aha, better late than never…my partner's now only a cauliflower, instead of the full cabbage I'd feared!"

"You said *you'd* fix it."

"And *you* said you'd raise the dosh."

"It'd be easier to raise the *dead* with my credit rating. The bank turned me down flat. Some mix-up about a letter they thought I'd sent. You haven't been writing to Captain Haddock at the A & E I suppose?"

"What are you on about?"

"It had something to do with fish anyway."

"Fish? You're babbling, man! Snap out of it."

"The name of the bank manager, you half-witted moron!"

"Just watch it, Goldman, or you'll find yourself on the fast train to Edgware General."

"What, me? Your old pal and business partner? The world's greatest detective, Hymie Goldman? You wouldn't threaten me, surely?"

"Good to see you're still full of it."

"Confidence?"

"Bull!" exclaimed Mike.

"Amounts to the same thing, Mike. So, where's the furniture?"

"On its way…good job one of us gets results. It should be here very soon so you'd better get a shave and brush up. You can't see Lady Muck looking like something the horse left in its stall."

"PIs are meant to look rugged and unkempt, Mike. You know, borderline disreputable."

"I know, but you're way over the border, mate. I wouldn't hire you to clean my bog, let alone baby-sit my prize racehorse!"

"Thanks for the testimonial. That bad, huh?"

"Believe it, dipstick."

"Okay, I'll get a shave. I still have that Remington Fuzz-Away somewhere; that should do it."

While Hymie was performing his ablutions a furniture van pulled up at the kerb outside. Artful Arnie had arrived.

"Oi, Murphy! You want this gear or wot?"

Mike ambled to the window, opened it and bawled out something that might have been "All right" and might not, but which certainly ended in "off"! When Hymie looked out onto the street moments later the two bruisers were deep in conversation.

"Need a hand, Mike?" he called down, without enthusiasm.

"You're in no state for lifting furniture, H, just leave it to the experts. Get yourself ready for the client."

Never the most enthusiastic devotee of physical labour, it didn't occur to Hymie to argue the point.

Mike returned from his discussions with their office-furnishings consultant and the two budding detectives adjourned to the Black Kat for a dose of warm grease and caffeine, while Arnie and his mate unloaded the van.

Returning half an hour later, replete, contented and basking in the warm glow of disaster averted, they stood on the threshold of their business premises waiting to be impressed at the last word in office chic arrayed before them. They needn't have bothered.

"What the flaming...!" said Hymie, struggling to give utterance to what they were both thinking.

The filing carousels and personal computer were nowhere to be seen, the workstations and swivel chairs were absent without leave and the architect of the chaos that remained was noticeable by his absence.

"I'll kill that toe rag, Arnie!" cried Mike, deeply moved.

They seemed to have been transported back in time to the days of the Roman Empire. Papier-mâché columns and colonnades jostled with plaster busts of minor deities and obscure emperors with aquiline noses. Ornate alabaster vases cluttered the surfaces and a linoleum mosaic of a hunting scene adorned the floor.

"We're knackered, H!"

"We don't have time to be knackered, Mike, the client will be here any minute. I've got to think of *something*. Something big. Something so crazy, so unbelievable that no one would bother to think it up!"

"Oh, yes, how silly of me not to have thought of it myself," said Mike. "We took this scenery in payment for a debt owed by a travelling theatre? No, too obvious...we've got a new way-out marketing strategy? I know...you think you're Julius Caesar! They're sure to believe that one!"

"You're not helping," said Hymie. "A lesser man would say it was all your fault."

"Shut it, Goldman. Face it, we're scuppered. We may as well stick a sign on the door, 'Gone Away', and head down the Job Centre."

"No way, Murphy. I've been in tighter scrapes than this. I can't immediately think of them, but I must have been. Keep the faith, we'll laugh about this one day."

"Yeah, the kind of hysterical laughter you produce just before the men in white coats wheel you away." It was clear that Mike wasn't used to putting a positive spin on disaster, unlike his business partner.

The bickering would no doubt have degenerated into a punch-up had not the sound of a woman's heels clicking down the passage outside brought them to their senses.

"Leave it to me," hissed Hymie.

"Good afternoon, Mr…"

It took a great deal to stymie Lucinda Hunting-Baddeley, but they had managed it within the first minute of their first meeting. Walking off the Finchley Road into ancient Rome was liable to do that to a person.

"Goldman, Hymie Goldman. I know what you're thinking," he said, with a hint of a smile.

"You do?" she replied.

"Yes, why the Roman stage scenery?"

"Exactly."

"Well, pull up a divan and I'll tell you. The answer is really very simple. A friend of mine runs an amateur theatre company nearby, The Strolling Players, putting on shows to raise money for charity, and one of his storage warehouses caught fire a few days ago. This was all they could salvage," said Hymie, gesticulating at the furniture.

"But why store it *here*?" asked Lucinda H-B.

"Well, it was in a good cause and I didn't think my clients would mind for a few days…bit of a novelty really."

She goggled at him momentarily and then simply caved in.

"Well, as long as there's an explanation, I suppose," she said, pulling up a divan.

"Naturally, madam. You don't think we make a habit of decorating the office like this, surely?" said Hymie, gaining in confidence as every minute passed without the loss of his new client.

"Well, as I've never met you before, I can hardly say, but I'm willing to give you the benefit of the doubt on this occasion, though surely your friend could have found some alternative storage space?"

"Unfortunately he was uninsured, so he won't even be able to replace the costumes and scenery he's lost. I just couldn't bring myself to turn him down when he asked for my help," said Hymie, with ringing sincerity.

"Good one," whispered Mike.

"And you would be?"

"I beg your pardon, Mrs Hunting-Badly, this is my junior partner and security consultant, Michael Murphy. He's currently working undercover, as am I; hence our appearance. We need to be able to move freely through some of the rougher districts of North London."

"Oh, I see. I *was* wondering. A high price indeed, Mr Goldman, being seen out in public like that. You will, of course, change your attire when you move into the stables, won't you? I won't have Lightning being put off his food by smelly clothes."

Mike raised his eyebrows in alarm. He wasn't about to ask too many questions of the client on first acquaintance, but it seemed to him that Hymie was already displaying a serious disregard for the principle of keeping him informed.

"Stables?" queried Hymie.

"Well where else would you expect to stay?" asked Lucinda Hunting-Baddeley. "You can't protect Lightning from kidnapping if you're staying in a hotel, now can you?"

"No, I suppose not," agreed Hymie, reluctantly.

"Sorry, Mrs er…who or what is Lightning?" asked Mike, who had been following some way behind the general drift of the conversation.

"Good heavens, Mr Murphy, I assumed you had been briefed on the assignment. I refer of course to Summer

Lightning, my championship racehorse. He's running in the Gold Cup you know. Well, I've received several threats through the post, telling me that if I don't scratch him from the runners' list something will happen to him."

"How dreadful," remarked Hymie.

"Precisely," agreed Mrs Hunting-Baddeley.

"Have you informed the police?" asked Mike.

"Well, yes, but they didn't seem to think they could do much about it until something had happened, by which time of course it would be too late. So I asked around to see if anyone knew of a good security firm and someone mentioned you."

Mike and Hymie eyeballed each other in silent disbelief.

"They said you were good with horses."

"You're sure it wasn't pigs?" asked Mike.

She looked perplexed. "Why would it be with pigs? Aren't you good with horses?"

"Just Mr Murphy's idea of a joke, I'm afraid," said Hymie. "I assure you we *are* good with horses. Very good in fact," he bluffed.

"Yes, Mr Goldman grew up on a farm and learned to ride at three," said Mike, sarcastically.

"Oh, where was that, Mr Goldman?"

"Out Hendon way," replied Hymie, with no trace of irony.

"I didn't realise they had farms out there," said their visitor.

"Yes indeed, but we mustn't let Mr Murphy hide his own light under a bushel," remarked Hymie. "He used to work in stables as a boy; mucking in and mucking out, all over the summer holidays. Mike the Mucker they used to call him. The horses loved him."

Mike glowered.

"Oh that *is* good to hear, Mr Goldman. I do so hope Lightning takes to you both. There'll be a nice bonus in it for you if he wins the Gold Cup."

"Ah, that reminds me," said Hymie, hurriedly. "We need to discuss our scale of fees."

She sized him up and took the measure of him in a glance. "A hundred pounds a day plus expenses?" she suggested.

"Each?" queried Mike.

"You drive a hard bargain," said Lucinda Hunting-Baddeley. She was kidding. Stuck in stables in the middle of nowhere there wouldn't be any expenses.

"It's a deal," said Mike. He couldn't face living in ancient Rome for long and his own flat had surely been repossessed by now.

"Good. Report for duty at two o'clock the day after tomorrow," said their new client. "Here's the address," she added, handing Hymie a card. She turned briskly on her heel and clicked off down the corridor.

"Let's get one thing straight, Mike," said Hymie. "*I* decide on how much we charge in fees. We could have held out for another fifty quid a week each!"

"So you say, mate. I just thought we needed a break."

Part Twenty-Eight

The convoy passed at a snail's pace, possibly slower. The traffic in this particular suburb of North London had been getting worse daily for years, to the point where it was now unquestionably quicker to walk. Quicker, but not safer. More accustomed to the soft leather upholstery of her Mercedes-Benz, Steffanie Scarlatti was going quietly insane in the back of the police van.

"Got a ciggie, sweetie?"

PC Reidy gazed at her in dumbstruck awe. He just couldn't accept the fact that this vision of loveliness was the murdering bitch everyone believed her to be.

"Go on, Officer, I'm gasping," she said.

It was he who was gasping. He drew out an open packet of cigarettes from his tunic pocket and offered her one. She smiled a devastating smile and took the packet.

"Got a light, Constable?"

He obliged. He would have liked to kindle another kind of fire in her but he was conscious of the irreconcilable gulf between them. Criminals were one species, law-enforcement officers another, and except in the course of duty never the twain should meet. It didn't quite work like that though, did it?

The clock crept on, imperceptibly slowly. Reidy's mind began to drift to his plans for later that evening. He thought of the barmaid in the Rose and Crown, a buxom blonde called Jenny. He'd been seeing her for a couple of weeks now. Maybe tonight would be his lucky night. About ruddy time too!

It wasn't to be. The grand orchestrator in the sky was on his tea break.

Outside the van flares began to explode, shrouding the convoy in a red mist and spreading their crimson rage across the grey sky. Visibility first reduced and then dwindled away to nothing.

Inside the van Steffanie Scarlatti lunged forward from her bench and stubbed out her smouldering cigarette in Reidy's face.

He doubled up in agony and screamed in a torrent of pain, but only momentarily before being battered unconscious against the side of the van. He slumped to the floor, was swiftly dispossessed of his handcuff keys, and had he been conscious and able to see through the fog, would have seen the object of his desire making a quick getaway down the street, aided and abetted by external allies with some serious industrial metal-cutters.

The escape hit the TV and radio news within the hour.

"The public are warned to be on their guard against escaped prisoner Steffanie Scarlatti...

"Scarlatti, aged twenty-five, height six feet, was last seen in Camden Town, North London, this afternoon, when a police van escorting her to Holloway Prison, pending committal proceedings for a range of offences including murder, was hijacked. The public are advised not to approach this woman. She is believed to be armed and is highly dangerous. Police have issued the following photofit picture. Anyone with information as to her whereabouts should contact the Metropolitan Police on 0845..."

Click! Lau pressed a button on his remote-controlled handset and Steffie Scarlatti was consigned to the airwaves. If only it were that simple.

"You have become something of a celebrity, Ms Scarlatti. Let me be the first to congratulate you," observed Lau.

"Save it, Lau. Celebrity has no value to me, you slitty-eyed reptile. It never pays to advertise *my* activities."

"As you wish. I didn't bring you here to discuss your personal popularity, or lack of it. We have arrangements to make. First, however, a word of warning: if you have the slightest idea of betraying my trust or murdering me in my bed, get rid of it now. Until you have completed our bargain you will be under constant supervision. Should that prove insufficient incentive, I need only remind you that I have a file on you so comprehensive it would guarantee your removal from society for an eternity. When they let you out you would be old and wrinkled and ugly and your future would be bleak." He knew exactly how to manipulate people to achieve maximum control.

"Don't try to threaten me, you withered old wreck!" Her bravado was simply for show, as she knew only too well.

"*Threaten* is an ugly word, and not one I care to use," continued Lau. "Nevertheless, the file is safely lodged with my lawyers in case I should meet with any unforeseen accident. My death or disappearance for more than a few days would certainly trigger its release to the authorities."

"Fine. What do you *want*, Lau?"

"You know what I want."

"Goldman and Timmins?"

"Just so. Goldman is about to start an assignment protecting a racehorse entered in the Cheltenham Gold Cup."

"You're kidding me." She smirked at the thought of Goldman protecting anything, when he could scarcely look after himself.

"No, I arranged it myself, through a gambling contact."

"What's the horse called?"
"Summer Lightning."
"And who is Edna Timmins?"
"One thing at a time. First Goldman, then we will talk of Timmins." Experience had taught Lau to be patient in all things.
"You can provide me with the necessary equipment?"
He passed her a business card. "This man will be your contact, Ms Scarlatti. He will provide you with guns, ammunition, anything you may need. I have arranged a meeting for Friday at ten-thirty. Be there."
"Is there anything else?"
"You don't need me to tell you your flat has police forensics crawling all over it."
"No."
"There is a room available for you on the first floor of this building, until you make other arrangements. Don't forget, you will be under surveillance until the assignment is complete."
She just nodded. She couldn't trust herself to speak to Lau any further. She would bide her time.

Part Twenty-Nine

The sun blazed down on the house and grounds of Baddeley Manor. Hymie and Mike had told the taxi driver to set them down at the entrance to the drive and were now regretting it. The drive seemed to stretch out forever.
"How long does a drive need to be?" speculated Hymie.
"Well, it's to keep the riffraff out, obviously."
"But we're here anyway," smirked Hymie.
"Maybe it's to keep out burglars."
"Well, possibly poor burglars who can't afford cars, but then they wouldn't get away very fast down *this* drive, would they? They could phone for the police to meet them at the gate."

"So maybe having a long drive is a good idea after all," said Mike.

"Tell that to my legs, they're almost dropping off with tiredness. I could swing for that ruddy Scarlatti woman. Destroyed my car, tried to kill me...and now leaves us to the mercy of public transport to get to the middle of nowhere." Hymie was nothing if not bitter and resentful. "Three trains, four buses, two taxis and now Shanks's pony."

"There goes today's wages!" cried Mike, wishing he'd left the negotiations to Hymie, so that at least he'd have someone else to blame.

"It's about time we got some new wheels, Mike. I know I'll never replace the Zebaguchi but I'm not cut out for all this exercise."

"I did notice a white transit on ebay recently for 99p. They said it needed some work doing, mind. The photo was very grainy too."

"I shouldn't wonder, but I think not. Still, we do need our own transport, especially now that Scarlatti's on the loose again. Did you hear about it on the radio?"

"I was with you when you heard about it, you plonker. Someone hijacked the van they were taking her to prison in. Makes you glad you're out of London for a few days, eh, H?"

"If you say so, Mike. Personally all this fresh air's getting on my nerves."

They finally reached journey's end, and passing through an elaborately carved wooden porch Mike pulled on an antique metal door-ringer, in the shape of the devil's head.

For what seemed an eternity nothing happened, and then, when they had almost given up hope, the door creaked open and an even creakier exhibit in butler's clothing greeted them. Jervis had been there so long he was listed in the house inventory: butler, one, clapped out. He displayed all the usual attributes of his anachronistic class – rotundity, sleekness, discretion, dignity and rabid loyalty, but in his case all of these things were overshadowed by forgetfulness bordering on the senile. He was, after all, on the old side of very old.

"Good afternoon, deliveries are round the back of the house, if you wouldn't mind," said Jervis, in the voice he reserved for tradesmen.

"We're Goldman and Murphy and we have an appointment with the lady of the house," said Hymie.

He looked dubiously at them, in a way suggesting they fell some way short of the guests he was used to dealing with. He retired to obtain further information, closing the door and shuffling off into the house. Outside everything remained quiet.

"Maybe he's died on us," quipped Mike, after another interminable wait.

"Don't make jokes like that, you may be right."

Mike rang the bell again.

Nothing happened.

He rang it again, repeatedly, and after a while the doddery old butler re-appeared, like some decrepit genie summoned from his lamp.

"Yes, can I help you?" asked Jervis, as though meeting them for the first time.

"We're here to see Lady Hunting-Baddeley. You were going to check whether we were expected," said Hymie.

"I was?"

"You were," Mike assured him.

"And your names are?" asked Jervis, scarcely crediting what they were saying.

"Goldman and Murphy!" they cried simultaneously.

"Perhaps we could wait *inside* this time, in case you forget us again," added Mike helpfully.

"Well, I'm sure I would have remembered *you two*," said Jervis, as if they were somehow subhuman. There was a trace of tetchiness in his voice, but he reluctantly let them in.

"Just a moment, please." He shuffled off into the house again, leaving the two of them to wait indoors for a change. They sat on carved wooden chairs and gazed around the reception hall, drinking in the ambience, the accumulations over centuries of occupation. On all sides were ancient oil paintings in heavy gilt frames. Here an eighteenth-century longcase clock, there an assemblage of antique porcelain. Mike started to pace up and down, stopping in front of an old family portrait to stare intently at the signature in the corner.

"It's a Bugrot," he declared, after much deliberation.

"Whoever heard of a Bugrot painting? Surely he did racing cars?" said Hymie dubiously.

"That was Bugatti, you great wally! Don't you know anything?"

"Well, I've never heard of an artist called Bugrot, you steaming great nit! Bugrot's what you get on your roses."

"You're having me on, H. When were you ever in a garden, except by accident?"

"Okay, okay, have it your way, Mike, I'm no Alan Titmarsh."

"Too true, but the painting's by Bugrot just the same. Come and have a look for yourself." They walked up to the heavy gilt frame.

"Must be the Dutch school," speculated Hymie, ignorantly.

"With a name like Bugrot? Danish, surely!"

"Hello, Mr Goldman, Mr Murphy." It was Lucinda Hunting-Baddeley. "I'm sorry to have kept you, gentlemen. Jervis came into the drawing room ten minutes ago, but it took him that long to remember what he came to tell me. Poor old chap. He's getting far too old for the job really, but they don't make butlers like him anymore. It would break his heart if I suggested he retire."

"Think nothing of it, madam, we were just admiring your Bugrot," said Mike, determined to get to the bottom of the artist's signature. He raised his eyes to the painting.

"Oh, the *Burgôt?* Yes, it's not a bad daub, don't you think? He's rather a promising French portraitist. It's a particular favourite of mine, as it's the only one I have of the entire family." She passed over Mike's embarrassment effortlessly.

Hymie might have known Mike's grasp of modern art would be less than slight, but chose not to undermine a junior partner in JP Confidential in front of their sole living client.

"I expect you'll want to see your charge now, won't you?"

"Charge? I thought *you* were paying *us*," said Mike.

"Summer Lightning, Mr Murphy."

"Of course," said Hymie, gesturing for Mike to shut up.

In short order they crossed the courtyard, entered the stable block, and were soon gazing intently into the large brown eyes of the most impressive racehorse either of them had ever seen. It was also the *only* racehorse either of them had ever seen, at least close up.

The horse looked distinctly unimpressed, as though he were being asked to shake hands with the village idiot and his less intelligent brother.

"Lightning, these are Mr Goldman and Mr Murphy. They've come to look after you for a few days," said the lady of the manor.

If he could have put his head in his hands, Lightning would have done so. He settled for shaking his head and showing his teeth.

"Well, I'll leave you to get acquainted. I'll send the head stable boy over to explain what's what." So saying, their hostess headed back to the house, leaving the pair wondering what they'd let themselves in for.

Hymie reached out to pat the horse's head and received a playful nip for his trouble.

"There, there, boy!" he said.

"I think he likes you," said Mike.

"I'd hate to see what he does to you if he doesn't like you."

"Hello, guys, I'm Jack, the head stable boy. I see you're getting to know Lightning. He's a great horse. He's all heart. Strong and fast too. We're expecting great things of him. Which one of you is Goldman, and which one's Murphy?"

"I'm Hymie Goldman," said H, holding out his hand in greeting.

"And I'm Mike Murphy." Mike eyed the newcomer with suspicion, as though he didn't trust anyone near Lightning.

"Welcome to the Hunting-Baddeley yard, guys. I gather you're with us until the Gold Cup, in charge of security, so I hear."

"Yes, that's the ticket, Jack," said Hymie.

"Mrs H-B tells me you know all about horses. That right?"

"Sure, I used to *ride on the farm at home*," Hymie said, looking daggers at Mike.

"Oh, right, you're from farming stock too. So am I. My family owns estates in Berkshire, how about yours?"

"Oh, just a caravan at Bognor."

He'd have to practise telling bigger lies, thought Hymie, as the words left his mouth. That was where real success lay. As it was, he just looked like a complete plonker.

"Well, you won't need *me* to tell you much, I don't suppose. All the grooming, feeding and exercising will be taken care of by the regular team. You guys just get to move into the stables for round-the-clock surveillance at other times, right?"

"Right!" said both. "Oh no!" they thought together.

"Oh, I was forgetting, we're a man down. Ted Farrell broke his foot the other day, and we need a driver to get Lightning over to his training camp for seven o'clock tomorrow morning. Think you can handle it? We'll help you load him into his box, of course. It's just over there at the back of the stables. I presume you're licensed to drive a truck?"

"Oh, ah, yes," said Hymie. "Bigger lies," he thought.

Mike looked a little doubtful.

"Great. Here's a map to the training ground. Don't forget, forty miles per hour max. Got it?"

"Of course, Jack, what do you take us for?" asked Hymie.

"Sure, I was forgetting. See you later, guys."

The evening and night passed slowly and uneventfully. As they were on duty they had their meals delivered on a tray – bacon, egg, beans and chips, which suited them admirably. Lightning soon got used to them and settled down for his shut-eye at about nine p.m. At eleven he started snoring and continued through much of the night.

Hymie and Mike kept watch in shifts until the early hours.

Mike seemed to be afflicted with hay fever, which kept him awake sneezing for much of the night, while Hymie spent his waking moments trying to develop a business plan for JP Confidential. The pile of wastepaper accumulating on the stable floor grew to impressive proportions, as he discarded one draft after another. Nevertheless he stuck at it, feeling sure that Ceefer Capital wouldn't be too impressed if he couldn't even tell them where he thought the business was going. He thought about calling Sarah Chandar, but wasn't sure what to say, and assumed she would take his call as a sign of weakness in any negotiations.

Morning broke over the stable yard. It was cold with a scattered frost on the fields. The two horse detectives awoke to their alarm clock at six a.m., grumbling among themselves.

Suddenly the ghostly form of Jervis the butler appeared before them, bearing a tray.

"Can I offer you breakfast, gentlemen?"

"Nothing could be better, Jervis. Thank you," said Hymie.

He laid the tray on the floor and hovered around.

"Care to join us, Jervis?" asked Mike.

"Oh no, sir, I've already eaten. I was wondering if I could assist you. Perhaps I could load Lightning into his box for you?"

"Well, it's very kind of you, Jervis, but Jack the lad did say he would come and give us a hand."

"Ah, I thought so, sir."

"Sorry, Jervis? What do you *mean*?"

"Well, he has a habit of playing practical jokes, sir. Far be it from me to criticise, but if I were you I would make alternative arrangements, sir. I myself know all there is to know about horseboxes and would be delighted to assist you."

"Thanks for the tip-off, Jervis. We'd be only too happy to take you up on your offer," chipped in Mike.

The butler shuffled off with Lightning in tow, disappearing down to the end of the stable block. Once outside he loaded a different horse with similar markings into the box, which he attached to the tow-bar at the back of the truck, and, lifting the truck's bonnet, cut through the brakes. He then loaded Lightning into the back of a transporter and quietly drove off in it.

Mike and Hymie demolished their breakfast oblivious to it all and then headed towards the far end of the stable block to join their benefactor.

"He's gone," said Mike, surprised.

"Strange or what?" Hymie was beginning to feel uneasy.

"Well, the horse is in the box and the keys are in the ignition," said Mike. "We've got the map from yesterday, so it looks like it's over to us now. You're driving I take it, H?"

"No, I thought you'd like to. It's the junior partner's privilege."

"I don't have a truck licence."

"Neither do I," Hymie assured him.

"So when you said…"

"I lied," said Hymie. "But how hard can it be, Mike? We can't go above forty mph anyway."

"On your head be it, H."

"You'll be fine. I have faith in you."

Mike drove. He crunched through the gears all down the driveway until they got out onto the open road, and then he gradually adjusted to this new motoring experience. The roads were mainly empty and the weather was glorious.

"Don't forget, keep to forty, Mike."

"This pile of junk won't do above thirty."

Hymie switched on the radio. Pavarotti was just reaching high C. "Nessun flamin' dorma! I don't believe it," cried Hymie, turning it off again.

"Rain's forecast for later," said Mike. "You wouldn't think it to look at that sunshine."

"It's always the way, sunshine one minute, rain the next. It's a bit like that old case of mine, the golden pig. One minute I had a gorgeous blonde client and a thousand quid in my pocket, the next everyone was dropping dead like flies all around me, and the police were trying to put the blame on me. You know, Mike, I've been thinking a lot about the golden pig lately."

"I thought you'd dropped the case since Lucy Scarlatti died."

"Well, yes…and no. I mean, it just seems completely wrong that her sister can get away with murder and theft. I'm sure she's got the pig."

"I'd steer clear if I were you, H. There's no percentage

in it. If you find the thing, it won't bring your client back, and Steffie's hardly gonna give it back."

"Did I tell you about the insurance reward, Mike?"

"What makes you think there is one?"

"Stands to reason. Someone must own the statuette and you wouldn't own something that valuable without either insuring it for megabucks or offering a substantial reward for its return." He could be remarkably sensible when he tried.

"You may be right, H."

"I'm sure of it. If we can find Steffie Scarlatti, the pig won't be far behind."

"Just be careful, eh, Hymie. She leaves a trail of death in her wake, that one."

"Oh, I'll be careful all right, Mike. Now then, according to these directions it's left just here."

Mike turned left. The road was a steep one. It seemed to fall away on an incline of one in ten. At first it was rather fun to be plunging downhill at forty miles per hour, but when they hit fifty, sixty and seventy, and Mike's foot hammered the brake pedal to no avail, they changed their tune.

"Aaaaaaarrghhhhh! Try the handbrake!" shouted Hymie.

"What do you think this is?!" cried Mike, handing him a piece of rusty metal.

The countryside sped past in a blur of green fields, blue skies and brown trousers. Time seemed momentarily to stand still, before speeding up exponentially.

KERRRASSHHH!

After the dust had settled, they found themselves listing to starboard at an angle of forty-five degrees, the mangled truck wedged firmly in a ditch. Hymie was troubled by a persistent ringing in his ears.

"Mike? Can you hear that noise? Mike!?"

"Uuurrggh! It's your mobile, you wally!" And so it proved.

"Hi there, Jim Diamond of *The Investigator* magazine here. Is that Hymie Goldman?"

"Hi, Jim, it's a bad time, I'm afraid, I've just been involved in an accident."

"Hymie, I can't hear Lightning! It's all gone eerily quiet," said Mike anxiously.

"Sorry to hear that, Hymie. I just wanted to tell you you've been nominated for an award in *The Investigator*'s annual awards ceremony."

"An award? Thanks, but what's it for?"

"Best use of technology – for your *website*, of course."

"Hold on a minute, Jim, have you been speaking to a lady called Sarah Chandar?"

"Yes, of course – she nominated you. But I did have a look myself, it's a *great* site. The interactive clue-identification game is a real winner."

Mike passed his finger in melodramatic fashion across his neck as though cutting his own throat, to get Hymie to end the call. Miraculously he took the hint.

"Thanks again, Jim. No offence but I have to dash, I've got a missing racehorse to find. I don't have access to the web just now anyway." He pressed the cancel button on his mobile and left Diamond puzzling over how a nominee for best use of technology couldn't access his *own* website.

"Sorry, Mike, you're right, we need to stick to the job in hand. You know, we're lucky to be alive after that crash. What happened?"

"Well, I put my foot to the floor and there weren't any flaming brakes, you plonker! Did you think I forgot to try them?"

"No, I mean *why* weren't there any brakes?"

"No idea. Look, let's get out of here before the petrol tank goes up, and while we're at it, let's see if we still have a champion racehorse, eh, H?"

They struggled to free themselves from their seatbelts. Hanging in mid-air didn't help. Mike managed to turn himself round to face the door, then kicked out at the battered panel until it finally burst open. He forced himself through the gap, jumped down and staggered around to the front of the vehicle to help free his partner through the broken windscreen. Their appearance had suffered, but they were relieved to find that their injuries were only superficial.

"Have a look in the horsebox, will you."

"Couldn't you? You're the senior partner after all. I seem to get all the cruddy jobs," lamented Mike.

"I don't like to. I'm a bit squeamish," confessed Hymie, lamely.

"Oh and I *love* looking at squished racehorses, I suppose?"

"Go on, Mike, I'll do it next time."

"If Lightning's dead or missing, mate, there won't *be* a next time. Word gets around like a flash."

"Well, all the more reason to go now." Hymie, although gutless, was persistent.

Mike should have known he wouldn't get any sense out of Goldman. Slowly the big man walked over to the horsebox and peered inside. It was empty. "No sign of a horse, H!"

"You're kidding," said Hymie, relieved.

"Take a look for yourself. There's a pile of man..."

"You're sure?"

"Positive," confirmed Mike.

"So, let's get this straight. We've *lost* the horse. We've *wrecked* the truck and horsebox, and we're stranded in the middle of nowhere. I can feel a new identity coming on!"

"I thought you were used to tough scrapes, Hymie. Yes, we've seemingly lost the horse, but it was hardly our fault. That truck was a complete *deathtrap*. Someone must have cut the brakes."

"I'm sorry, Mike. I'm just a bit upset. I know you think I've got no nerves, but I have. It's all starting to get on top of me. You're probably right about the brakes."

"I'm sure of it. No one said this job was going to be a walk in the park. Some serious villains are planning to stop Lightning from racing and they're not about to let us get in their way. So let's show them we mean business. First of all, we've got to find Lightning before someone else does."

"You never said a truer word, Mike," said Hymie, the light of battle gradually returning to his eyes. "So, what's your plan?"

"Plan? Ah, well...we could walk around calling out his name."

"A bit lame, isn't it?"

"...or we could phone the police, to see if anyone's returned a racehorse to lost property?"

"Lamer still," added Hymie. "Well, I'm all for shouting out his name."

"And the police?"

"The trouble is, we don't own the horse so we'd have a job to explain what we were doing looking for it, and if we told them, the first thing they'd do is call Lady Hunting-Baddeley, and then we'd be sunk – we could wave goodbye to our fee for starters. If we can find Lightning we may be able to retrieve the situation. Besides, how would you describe the horse? Big with brown eyes?"

"Does he have brown eyes?"

"Call yourself a detective?"

"Not often," he conceded.

"I'm not surprised," said Hymie, "but the fact remains that it's a rotten idea. Got any other winners?"

"We could hire some *real* detectives to find him," said Mike, provocatively.

"*Real* detectives?! Listen, Mike, *we're* real detectives! Anyway, can you imagine explaining to them why we need their services? We'd be a laughing stock. We have to find the horse ourselves."

"Lightning, Lightning! Here, boy!" shouted Mike.

"I admire your willingness to make a complete fool of yourself in a crisis, but this is a *racehorse* we're looking for. He could be halfway across the country by now. We'll never find him on foot."

"That's where you're wrong, mate," said Mike. "Don't you know anything about horse psychology? Given the choice between running halfway across the country and having a good nosh-up, he'll take the nosh-up every time."

"Thank you, James Herriot. That's your expert opinion, is it?"

"Gotta be worth a try."

They ambled along the lane, Mike checking the left-hand side of the road and Hymie the right. "Lightning! Lightning!"

they chorused, like a couple of drunks looking for their car keys. They wandered the length and breadth of the area until they arrived at the nearby village of Southam, where they accosted a succession of passers-by with one recurrent question:

"Excuse me sir/madam/sonny, have you seen my racehorse?"

"No, what's he look like?" seemed to be the perennial response.

They passed pretty stone cottages, a pub (which took some doing), and a small ruined castle, before finally arriving at the red telephone box outside the church of St Swithin's. They had all but given up the search and started thinking wistfully about the pub when a large chestnut gelding appeared, as if by magic, from the front garden of a nearby cottage.

"Lightning. Here, boy," said Mike, calmly.

A little girl with pigtails appeared from the far side of the horse as it stooped down to nibble on a geranium. "Do you like my horse, mister?"

"He's a very fine horse, young lady, how clever of you to find him," said Hymie.

"'Ere, H, you sure it's him?" queried Mike, cautiously.

"Of course I'm sure," he hissed.

Hymie and Mike led the racehorse back down the lane with the little girl calling after them, "Come back, Sugar Lump, you're a bad horsy, leaving me on my own. Come back and play!"

Relief surged over them. They could hold their heads up high again. Yes, they may have lost the truck and horsebox, due to the sabotage of some would-be horsenappers, but they had saved Summer Lightning. He would race at Chelters, come what may.

Part Thirty

All great detectives had to brief their staff, and Inspector Ray Decca was no exception. "I'll keep it short, ladies and gents..."

It would certainly be that; he had practically nothing new to say.

"As the Bard said, 'an honest tale speeds best, being plainly told'."

A chorus of disapproval swept through the briefing room.

"Have you noticed, he always quotes Shakespeare when he's got nothing to go on," observed Sergeant Shorthouse. "It's a diversionary tactic."

"That'll do. Right, cast your minds back to last Tuesday 3rd March. It's 4.15 in the afternoon. A prison van containing Steffanie Scarlatti is on its way to Holloway. En route it gets hijacked. It was a professional job – smoke grenades, metal-cutters, the works. They didn't know what hit them. Ask Reidy. She was sprung from the van and disappeared in this area, here on the map in quadrangle A."

He pointed with an old PT drill stick at an enlarged street map he'd Blu-Tacked to the wall, to emphasise the point.

"We divided the area into six zones, denoted on the map by letters alpha through foxtrot."

"Any particular reason, Chief?"

"We always use alpha through foxtrot," chipped in Shorthouse.

"Thank you, Sergeant, I'm coming to that, Terse. We had forensics all over the crime scene, we conducted a thorough door-to-door search of the area, we brought in every grass and petty thief for miles around and gave them the third degree, but no one was talking. They were all scared. We have about as much to go on as a holidaymaker on a French campsite."

"Nicely put, Chief. Except, where's Moffat Road?" asked Sergeant Terse.

"Moffat Road? Why this strange babbling about Moffat Road, Terse?"

"It's on your map, Chief, as bold as brass, but I've never seen it and I grew up around there," said the methodical sergeant.

The great man screwed up his eyes and scratched his head.

Where *was* Moffat Road? It wasn't anywhere he knew. Suddenly the explanation dawned on him.

"Ahem, well spotted, Terse. I was waiting to see who'd get there first. This, of course, is a street plan of Dumfries, left over from that strategic policing lecture Jock McTavish gave last week. The moral is...always expect the unexpected.

"Okay, we haven't found Steffanie Scarlatti yet," he resumed, "but we're going to. I can't believe she would leave her home territory in a hurry, so we're going to keep on doing what we've been doing and wait for her to make a mistake. Does anybody have any suggestions? Henderson?"

"We could follow up the nightclub connection, sir. Scarlatti is known to be an active clubber."

"Good. Of course, we've checked out the club where she used to gamble; the Rainbow Rooms, but as you say, she was a keen club-goer and there must be hundreds, maybe thousands of private members' clubs around. Terse, you and Henderson get on to all the cab firms – see if any of them remember dropping off a woman of her description at a club in the last week or two. Circulate the photofit. She's an attractive woman, surely someone must remember her."

"Aye aye, Chief, are you an admirer?" asked Sergeant Terse with a grin.

"Certainly not, Terse."

"We also know the Rainbow Rooms are a front for the Triads, sir, perhaps she has links with them?"

"Yes, Henderson, good point. We don't know too much about her involvement with the Triads, but it's certainly an area to explore. Perhaps she knew something they wanted to keep under wraps and sprang her to silence her, or perhaps she's working for them. There are numerous possibilities."

"If you're right, Chief, I don't envy those Chinks!" said PC Jackson.

"Too true. Reidy's still in intensive care. Don't be fooled by her glamour-model looks, she's poison. If you do come up against her, don't take any chances – let her have it with your truncheon."

"You do fancy her, Chief!"

"Shut up, Terse, this is neither the time nor the place," snapped Inspector Decca.

"What about Interpol, Chief?"

"Not now, Jackson."

"I meant, wouldn't they have a file on her, sir?"

"Good thinking, but I doubt she's known outside the UK. Follow it up anyway."

"Will there be another press conference today?" asked Henderson.

"Jack Daniels is handling it, folks, but heaven knows what he's going to say."

"Sir, Chief Superintendent Morrison wants to see you in his office."

"Thanks, Suzy. Sergeant Terse will conclude this briefing. The real street plans must be in my office, Terse. Give me an update later, all right?"

"Certainly, Chief."

"Ah, Ray, come in, sit down. I've been meaning to have a word with you. I'm concerned at the lack of progress on the Scarlatti case. It's bad for morale having a murderer loose on the streets. Where the blazes is she? It's not as if she's invisible and yet she seems to have disappeared off the face of the planet. Do you think she's left the country or is someone harbouring her? More to the point, what are you doing about it?"

"Everything possible, sir. I've just had a team briefing on it. We've tried door-to-door, forensics and every grass and petty crook for miles around. No one knows anything. We're still pursuing a few leads though."

"What leads?" asked Chief Superintendent Morrison, irritably. If his golf handicap began to slide it would take months to recover and he held Inspector Decca personally responsible.

"We know she's a keen clubber..."

"Yes, she's very violent, I know."

"...so we're checking out all the clubs and taxi firms in the area."

"Ah, yes."

"We're also exploring possible links with the Triads, sir." He wondered if Morrison even knew what a Triad was.

"That's all very well, Decca, but we need results, man, *results*, not leads. Have you spoken to Scotland Yard and the Drug Squad lately? Or Interpol, come to that?"

"We're working on it, sir." Decca knew it sounded lame, but it was the best they could do.

"What were you saying about the Triads?"

"Scarlatti used to work at the Rainbow Rooms' casino, a well-known haunt of the Chinese gambling fraternity. As you know, sir, the croupier Tony Lee turned up dead not half a mile from there, and the victim of that other gangland killing, Tony Martino, had rumoured links with the Triads."

"Sounds like they've got it in for people called Tony. Makes you glad your name's Ray, eh?"

How could an idiot be a chief superintendent, wondered Decca?

"Lee was also a known associate of Scarlatti's," added the inspector.

"I see. Murky waters, eh, Ray?"

"Word on the street is that the Rainbow Rooms is a front for all kinds of illegal activity – drug pushing, pornography, illegal firearms."

"Then why the blazes haven't you shut it down? You could have suspended their gaming licence or kept raiding the place until no one went near the place. Strike at their home base and they'll scurry off somewhere else, Ray."

"Insufficient evidence, sir. It's the old, old story. The Drug Squad's after Mr Big, but all they can do is finger the couriers, so they drag a few of them into court and it stops nothing. They keep trying to get a man on the inside, but don't seem able to pull it off. Martino or Lee could've been undercover for all we know, they just don't keep us properly informed."

"Which Triad are we dealing with, do we know?"

"Not for sure, sir. We think there are at least a dozen operating in the UK. They tend to stick to their own territories. There are three in Liverpool and Greater Manchester, two in Glasgow and maybe six in London."

"That's only eleven."

"There's one known to be operating in Gloucestershire, centred on Cheltenham, sir."

"Is nothing sacred!" cried Morrison, who had family there.

"Seemingly not, sir."

"How much information do we have on their activities?"

"Not enough. So far there's been a real lack of political will to do anything about it. We need to set up the kind of organised crime task forces they have in Hong Kong and the States." Decca sounded like an old campaigner, climbing onto his trusty soapbox.

"Have you made any approaches in the right quarter, Ray?"

"I've spoken to the Director of Operations of the OCTB in Hong Kong, a guy called Eddie Hu."

"Who?"

"Yes, sir, Eddie Hu."

"You're kidding, right?"

"No, sir, I'm Decca. Wright transferred to traffic last month."

"Get out of here, Decca, and for heaven's sake let's get a result quickly, or you'll never make chief inspector."

Part Thirty-One

They made a pathetic sight; two lumbering, rain-sodden deadbeats, being led down the drive of Baddeley Manor by a racehorse. Even now, it had failed to dawn on them that it was the *wrong* racehorse.

Jervis smirked from an upstairs window, and awaited the onset of the fun and games with anticipatory glee. The front doorbell rang in the distance but he carried on adjusting the sights on his telescopic umbrella. He wasn't about to answer any more doors for those two low comedians. With practised ease he unscrewed the silencer unit and slid it back into its casing in the handle. It was approaching the dénouement of this sorry little saga, and then his mission would be at an end. Having completed his checks he put the umbrella under his arm and headed for the back staircase, leading down to the stable block.

Lucinda Hunting-Baddeley had been planning the weekend menus with Cook when the doorbell rang for the first time, but having now finished, and with no sign of Jervis, she reluctantly opened the door herself.

"Mr Goldman! Mr Murphy! Whose horse is this?"

They were too demoralised to register the least concern.

"The truck broke down on the way to the training camp!" moaned Hymie.

"But where's Lightning?"

"Someone cut the brakes! We were nearly killed!" cried Mike.

"What have you done with my racehorse?!"

"This is it. Don't you even recognise your own horse?"

"Lightning has a white flash on his left fetlock, Mr Goldman. This animal has one on his *right* fetlock. Surely you must have noticed?"

"This is the horse your butler loaded into the box. I don't know what the world's coming to if you can't trust your own butler," said Hymie, bitterly.

"Whether he did or not is neither here nor there. This creature *isn't* Lightning. Where *is* Lightning?"

Hymie gaped at her speechlessly for a moment. "When did you last see him?"

"Yesterday, of course. What have you done with my racehorse, you blithering idiot?" She seemed to be verging on hysteria.

"You said that already. Have you tried the stables? Maybe he never left this morning? Maybe he's a homing racehorse?" suggested Hymie. Mike remained silent like a defendant exercising his right not to incriminate himself.

"I'll ignore your impertinence, but you had better be right. He had better be in the stables or it will be a dark day for JP Confidential, I assure you. Let's go and see, shall we." It was neither a suggestion, nor a request, but a command. You had to admire her in full flow, thought Hymie, wishing it was with someone else. They filed out across the driveway to the stable block.

"Jack! Jack!" called Lucinda H-B.

"Yes, ma'am?"

"Is Lightning in his stall?"

"No, ma'am, I haven't seen him since late last night. I assumed he was at his training camp by now. These gents were meant to be escorting him."

"That's all I wanted to know. Phone for the police, Lightning has been kidnapped!"

"Kidnapped? But!" He seemed genuinely taken aback, but Hymie was beginning to suspect everyone.

"I know, but let's hope it's nothing worse than that, Jack."

"Hey, what about my fee?" said Hymie, trying to keep a grip on what *really* mattered.

"*Our* fee!" cried Mike, thinking the same thing.

"Jack, show these prize idiots to the dining room until the police get here. As for your fee, you can whistle for it! I hope you have a good insurance policy, gentlemen, because you're going to need it."

Hymie had had enough.

"So, sue us. I'm sure we have an equally strong case against you, Mrs Snotty. That truck was a *deathtrap*. You could find yourself facing a charge of attempted murder, or at least manslaughter."

"I'll give *you* manslaughter, you pathetic little man!" snapped Lucinda Hunting-Baddeley.

"Quick, Mike, run for it!"

They turned tail and fled. It wasn't so much the thought of their aggrieved client as the prospect of being questioned by the police again that was exercising their minds.

It seemed that Hymie was destined to accumulate ever more impossible cases, until he could break the spell by solving one. He meant to find Summer Lightning and bring Steffanie Scarlatti to justice, if only to lay his own ghosts to rest, but to do it he would need to get back to North London. Nothing seemed to make any sense out in the wilderness of the countryside.

Part Thirty-Two

Nowhere on earth looks more out of sorts, more sorry for itself than a second-rate nightclub during daylight hours. This was particularly true of Leptospirosis. What passed for street credibility in the dark became undisguised squalor under the sun's merciless rays.

Sergeant Barry Terse simply didn't register the exterior décor. He was no limp-wristed makeover ponce off the telly, he had a proper job to do. No one could accuse him of prevaricating about the bush, he just swaggered up to the front door and pummelled it with a ham-like fist.

His junior colleague, Potter, on the other hand saw himself as a frustrated Thespian in policeman's clothing. He preferred to stand a little downstage of the action, particularly when it became violent, and visualise a kind of personal karma with whatever assignment he'd been given. In Terse's book he was a complete wally.

To Terse this assignment was simply one of a) getting into the club and b) finding out if the scum who ran this dive knew where that slapper Scarlatti was hiding. Modern policing had passed him by. In fact, it had given him a wide berth, not wishing to get its head kicked in.

"Come on, pansy, let's get this show on the road."

"After you, Sarge. How shall we play it?"

"That's your trouble, Potter, you're always playing at something. This is police work, not the Old Vic."

"But, what's my *motivation*?"

"What, pay cheque not enough for you?" asked Terse. "Okay, have it your way. I'm sure you've seen the repeats of *Starsky and Hutch* and all those other old American buddy-buddy shows. Well this week we're going to play good cop, bad cop."

"One of us is a mean son-of-a-bitch and the other one's as nice as apple pie?"

"Yeah, that's the general idea, Potter."

"Which is which, Sarge?"

"Well, I know what you're thinking. We should play to type, so I'm going to give you a challenge...you can be the bad cop. You should be able to handle that, eh?"

Potter looked a little hesitant.

"Got it, Sarge. I'm the bad guy, you're the good guy, right?"

"Exactly."

Potter seemed to collect himself together momentarily, then charged at the door to resume the battering Terse had already started to inflict on it.

"Open up, scum! Open up, d'yer hear?!" cried PC Potter, ambitiously.

The door opened slowly and a massive bouncer poked his head around it. He had the appearance and bearing of King Kong coupled with the warmth and charm of Attila the Hun.

"About ruddy time, you great spawny-eyed wassock! Get me the manager, and be quick about it!"

Potter flashed his police badge at the human obstruction, lest the bouncer should think he was just looking for a fight. He was showing a game streak Terse wouldn't have given him credit for. It was Terse's turn.

"Excuse my colleague, sir; he's of an excitable disposition. Could we just have a quiet word with the manager, please? Tell him Sergeant Terse and PC Potter of the Metropolitan Constabulary would be grateful for his co-operation."

"Get lost, filth!" said the bouncer.

"I don't think you heard the sergeant properly, fatso. Get the manager immediately or I'll kick your ass from here to Timbuktu!"

"Just try it, ponce!"

"Please, gents, please. We're all reasonable men here. There's no need for any trouble. I'm sure we can sort this out without resorting to abusive language and violence." Inspector Decca would have been proud of him, thought Terse.

"Which part of 'Get lost, filth!' didn't you understand, you morons?"

"Now, now, sir, there's no need for that language." The sergeant was enjoying this.

The bouncer looked at Terse as though he had just arrived from another planet. He cast an appraising eye over the opposition; two bog-standard coppers, no iron bars, no baseball bats, no knives. He could take them any time he felt like it, without so much as breaking into a sweat. Now was as good a time as any. He took a swipe at Potter.

Potter saw a hefty fist approaching him at about twenty-five miles per hour, and started to duck. His instincts were good, but his response time just wasn't fast enough and he caught the tail of the hurricane on the side of his head. He spun round and fell to the ground, groaning.

Terse had had enough of play-acting. He stomped on the partly open door and it crunched onto the bouncer's knee, bringing him down to Terse's level. Then he followed through with an instinctive uppercut to the chin.

Ordinarily that would have been enough, but Fat Jock was a bouncer made of sterner stuff. Grimacing through the pain he recovered sufficiently to land a couple of juicy wallops on Terse's coconut-like head.

"OOF! OOF!!" exclaimed the sergeant, involuntarily. "I don't believe you wanted to do that, sir," said Barry Terse, through clenched teeth.

He withdrew his truncheon with practised ease and smacked the bouncer smartly twice across the head.

THWACK! THWACK!!

The sound reverberated like an old growth tree being felled in the primeval forest, and the lumbering doorman went down like a detonated chimney stack.

Terse stepped delicately over the big man and walked into the club, through reception, past the cloakrooms, across the dance floor bedecked with a retro glitter ball, and up to the door marked "Strictly Private". He opened it and walked in.

"Is the manager in, love?" he enquired of the little old lady within.

Edna Timmins looked the sergeant over for a moment before dismissing him as a creature of minimal intellect.

"No, he's out." She lifted a black bin bag and emptied the wastepaper basket into it. "I'm the cleaning lady.

There's no one else here yet, but didn't the doorman tell you that?"

"I think he had other things on his mind."

"Can I take a message?"

"Just tell him Sergeant Terse was looking for him."

"Was there anything else?"

"Only that if he doesn't call me back today I may have to pay him another visit when the club's open. Oh, and you'd better phone for an ambulance, there's an injured policeman outside. I don't know – these young coppers are very accident-prone."

She lifted the phone and called for the ambulance. There was more to him than she had first thought. Oh yes, he was certainly stupid, but brave and dedicated for all that.

Anyone who could get the better of Fat Jock was no slouch with his fists either. She was going to need to up the stakes from now on.

Part Thirty-Three

Ray Decca was always in a bad mood after an interview with Sergeant Terse. The man was simultaneously an incorrigible idiot and the best man he had on his team, and he could never decide which of the two had the upper hand from one minute to the next.

Give the man a routine enquiry and there would be bodies piled up everywhere in no time. The episode at Leptospirosis was just the latest in a long list of examples. Yet give him something difficult to do and he would sail through it like a small child programming a DVD recorder. It was this eternal contrariness that drove Decca mad.

The phone on his desk started ringing.

"Decca."

"Morrison here. Can you spare me a minute? I have Charlie Chow of the Organised Crime and Triad Bureau in my office. I thought you should hear his briefing at first hand."

"Ordinarily, sir, I'd be delighted, but I've rather an important domestic matter to sort out first," said Decca, apologetically.

"Domestic matter? Poppycock, man! I need you in on this one, Decca."

He could see that it wasn't going to be easy. "To be frank, sir, it's Sheila."

"Sheila?"

"My wife, sir."

"Ah, yes."

"We've been going through a rough patch lately, what with all the overtime on the Scarlatti case. I've got an appointment at the Marriage Guidance Council this afternoon. Sheila is counting on me being there."

"I sympathise, Decca, but you must appreciate that this is a unique opportunity to talk openly with a specialist in Triad operations. I won't order you to attend but I'll take a pretty dim view if you choose not to. I'm sure you can rearrange your appointment."

"I'll speak to Sheila, sir." Even as he said it he knew he wouldn't, that he couldn't face her. Whatever it said on his marriage certificate, he was married to the job.

Chow was a slightly built, Hong Kong Chinese who smoked something that smelt like dope (but couldn't be, surely?). It was all part of his public persona.

Decca offered him his hand. "Ray Decca, Inspector, CID."

"Pleesed to meet yu, Inspector Sid, Charlie Chow, Ho Cee Tee Bee."

It sounded like gibberish until he realised that Chow was referring to the "OCTB" or Organised Crime and Triad Bureau.

"No, Decca – Ray Decca."

"Charlie was just telling me about the Ho Wop Do, Decca."

It sounded like a doo-wop number from the 1970s and reminded him of the last time he and Sheila had been dancing together.

"Ho Wop Do, sir?"

"Apparently the name of the Triad operating in the Cheltenham area."

"So our sources were correct," said Decca.

"Sauces, Hinspector?" queried Chow, thinking of lunch.

"Oh, just some local reports, Charlie."

"Eddie Hu asked me to give you a bliefing, Chief Superhintendent Mollison," said Chow, like a grotesque parody of himself.

"A bliefing?" queried Morrison.

"Solly, sir, I must get these dentures fixed," explained Charlie Chow.

"It would appear, Decca, that Cheltenham is in the control of the Ho Wop Do. They have moved in and taken over all the illegal rackets going, and set up a few that weren't," said CS Morrison, gravely.

The diminutive Mr Chow affixed a piece of Blu-Tack to the back of his dental plate, re-inserted it and continued:

"That's better. The Ho Wop Do, or Hodo, was set up in Hong Kong by a mysterious figure called Leslie Chang, commonly known as the Baron. No one knows for sure what he looks like, though his codename in Hodo is King Prawn as he's very partial to seafood. As you know, when Hong Kong reverted to China in 1997 many of the Triads relocated to the USA – San Francisco, Los Angeles, even San Diego. The Baron went to Cheltenham."

"No sense of direction eh? So why did this guy Prawn Cracker or whatever choose Cheltenham?" asked Morrison.

"He's a racing fanatic and a big-time gambler. The other rackets – the drugs, pornography and tiddlywinks super league – were all run to secure funds for his gambling obsession.

"Men like him live to gamble, and as his favourite race was always the Gold Cup he made the customary political donations and set himself up there in a luxury Regency apartment."

"Tell us more about the rackets they run. What are they up to?" asked Decca.

"What *aren't* they up to would be nearer the mark. I

wouldn't put it past them to try to fix the Gold Cup itself, by any means possible."

"What, nobble the favourite?" queried Morrison, aghast.

"Certainly. Then there are the betting scams, kidnapping, horsenapping, catnapping and washing dirty money."

"You mean laundering," Decca corrected.

"Yes, that too. Chinese laundries are big business. Then of course there's dentures," continued Chow.

"Good God, man! They haven't infiltrated the British Dental Association! Is nothing sacred?" Chief Superintendent Morrison was by now in a state of high anxiety.

"'Dentures' is the codename for drugs, sir."

"Of course. I knew that, Ray, what do you take me for?"

"So this King Prawn character, what front is he using in Cheltenham? Presumably they also run legitimate businesses?"

"Oh, the usual stuff, Chinese restaurants, a hotel or two, and the casino."

"And in Prestbury Park itself?" queried Morrison.

"You can be sure he has an inside team, especially on race days," confirmed Chow.

"Who's in it?" Ray Decca had already forgotten his appointment with Sheila.

"It could be anyone. The bookies, the jellied-eel-sellers, the catering franchise-holders, the bar staff, you name it."

"Can you give us the names and *modus operandi* of any members of the Ho Wop Do operating in the area?"

"I'll gladly share my files on those suspected of being in the UK," said Charlie Chow.

"Thanks, Charlie," said Decca. "It seems to me the immediate concern is the stable yards in the run-up to this year's Gold Cup. Do the Triads run their own?"

"For sure, Inspector, but we can watch *them*. The bigger challenge is what they get up to in *other people's* yards."

"They bribe trainers and stable hands then?"

"They own them," said Chow, simply.

"It looks like my overtime costs will be going through the roof again this month," thought Decca, irritably.

Part Thirty-Four

"I'd like sausage, eggs, bacon, toms, mushies, beans – oh, and some fried bread," said Mike.

"And to drink?" asked the waitress.

"Tea with four sugars."

"And you...?" She had been about to call him "sir" before she caught sight of Hymie and decided you could stretch a point, or a word, only so far.

"The same, but with black coffee."

The waitress turned back to the serving hatch.

"Two cardiac specials, Harry!"

They sat in the Black Kat after what seemed days of travel on public transport.

"It's good to be home...or nearly home anyway," said Hymie. "I thought we'd better get some grub before returning to the office, Mike. I can't face ancient Rome at this time of day on an empty stomach."

"Know whatcher mean, H. Things haven't been too rosy lately, have they? I don't half miss being a bouncer. I'd wake up around noon, have a full English breakfast and do nothing for the rest of the day until it was time to check in at the club. Then I'd get a bit of exercise chucking people out and before you'd know it, it was time to go home again. Even the traffic was lighter on the graveyard shift." A wistful look flitted across his granite features.

"Don't you start, Mike! People are forever prattling on about the good old days. Take the '60s. They reckon if you can remember them, you weren't there, as if that sounds impressive. What a load of garbage!"

"Oh I dunno, the music was better then," said Mike, defensively.

"Are you kidding? It's collective brainwashing. Cliff Richard? The Stones? Absolute tosh. As for the Beach Boys, I'd rather have a heap of manure dumped on my swivel chair than listen to another track from *Pet Sounds*. It's all dreadfully overrated and I really object to still having the geriatric perishers foisted on us at every turn. Just because the only people who can afford to go to concerts and buy CDs anymore are middle-aged." Hymie was incensed.

"Like yourself, you mean? Only *with cash*, obviously. I was forgetting you're such a cool dude, H, but I don't think any of the '60s legends you've got it in for will lose much sleep over it. They're laughing all the way to the bank."

"Even the food was worse then. No choice of takeaways at all: it was chips or nothing, no Kentucky Fried Chicken, no McDonalds, and if you'd asked for a pizza, they'd have said 'Piece of *what*, mate?' No, the '60s should be sealed in a lead canister and buried somewhere with instructions not to be re-opened until after I'm dead."

"That soon, H? Well, I don't care what you say, I quite liked that 'Livin' Doll'."

Hymie looked at him in disbelief.

"Yeah, and people were friendlier and there weren't so many ruddy foreigners in London."

"You're kidding, right? London's always been full of foreigners," said Hymie. "Who else do you think would be daft enough to live here? Besides, I suppose Murphy's an old cockney name, eh? I expect your granddad came over to avoid the potato blight."

"What, in 1953?"

"Researched your family tree, have you, Murphy?"

"'Ere, Goldman, just watch your mouth. This is my hometown and I won't hear you or anyone else badmouthing it. Got it?"

"It's mine too, but it doesn't mean I have to like it, Mike. Maybe if we were rich we'd enjoy living here, but as it is, it's just a relentless battle against insurmountable odds. I'm gonna make my pile and get out. Somewhere warm and sunny with lots of scantily clad women in skimpy grass skirts."

"Dream on, H."

The cardiac specials arrived and the conversation ended momentarily as they topped up their cholesterol levels, which had threatened to fall dangerously low.

"You can't beat a good fry-up," said Hymie, tucking in.

"You won't get an argument on that, H."

Shortly afterwards they adjourned to the decadent offices of JP Confidential, full of beans and ready for whatever life had in store. As usual it was a toss-up between raining stones and hailing daggers. An eviction notice had been nailed to the door, while inside on the mat lay several days' worth of final reminders, free papers and a postcard from Australia.

"He's only gone and flown out to Australia, the pillock!" cried Hymie, aggrieved.

"Who?"

"Benny Baker, that's who."

"Well, what's wrong with that? It looks like a great place on all the holiday programmes," said Mike. "Have you seen this card? 'Greetings from Bondi Beach'. Just look at that lady lifeguard; she can save me any day."

"What's wrong is, he's gone out to visit his brother Syd."

"So? I'm not with you."

"He hasn't *got* a brother Syd. It was me. I went to see him in Edgware General and had to tell them I was his brother, visiting from Australia, to get in to see him. Only he was in such a state that he actually believed me."

"I don't buy it, H. I reckon he's just using that load of old pony as a cover story for taking his favourite waitress out on a long-haul jolly."

"And who might that be?"

"Susie Parker, of course, the blonde with the forty-inch bust."

"I can't say I've noticed," said Hymie, with a far-away look in his eyes.

"Prepared to take a lie detector test?"

"No chance. So what does he say on his card?" he asked, changing the subject to spare his blushes.

"He says he hasn't managed to find Syd yet."

"No kidding!"

"That he's having a marvellous time with Susie and that he may not come back."

"*Never?*" Hymie's world seemed to wobble on its very

foundations at the thought of life without Benny's mouth-watering pizzas.

"And he goes on to say you can have first refusal on Benny's Bakery."

"He's selling up, eh? Well, I won't deny I've always fancied myself surrounded by mouth-watering grub – but as the proprietor?"

"Your real forte is as a *consumer*, H. Stick to what you're good at: eating."

"You're probably right, Mike. At least that's more in my price range."

Mike opened the front door and removed the eviction notice. "What are we going to do about this, *partner*? Without the money we could well find ourselves out on the street. According to this notice we have seven days to cough up £5,000 plus interest. In fact, H, it was dated two days ago, so we actually only have *five* days."

"Seven days? Five days? It's all the same – nigh on impossible. Is there anything left worth taking or shall we just do a runner now? I expect I should take the oil lamp for old times' sake, but it's hardly likely to be worth anything."

There was a knock at the door.

"Parcel for Mr Goldman. Sign here, please." The courier seemed to be in a hurry.

Hymie took the box and signed for it.

"Funny, but how would anyone know I was going to be here at this precise moment?"

"I couldn't tell you, is it from *Reader's Digest*? What's wrong with a parcel once in a while anyway? As long as it's not ticking." Mike smirked.

"Funny you should say that, buddy, but I *can* hear a faint ticking sound," said Hymie.

"Well, we don't have a clock, I don't have a watch and..."

"Mine is broken."

"Run!! Chuck it out of the window, now!!"

Hymie ran to the nearest window, undid the catch and dropped the box. Before it hit the pavement it exploded.

KABOOOOMMM!!!

The walls shook dramatically. All the windows of 792A, B and C Finchley Road shattered and migrated across a wide area in a tidal wave of glittering destruction, scattering damage, injury and pain indiscriminately in their wake. Goldman and Murphy, instinctively leaping facedown onto the cracked lino of their first-floor office, received only assorted flesh wounds.

They shook themselves back into the land of the living and made a hasty retreat down what was left of the fire-escape ladder.

However stunned and shaken they may have felt, past experience had taught them that being questioned by the police wouldn't make them feel a whole lot better. Mike cautiously scanned the street for would-be assailants, but fleetingly saw only the back of an old guy, resembling none other than their recent acquaintance, Jervis the butler.

"Nah, get a grip," he thought to himself. "You're not a popular guy, H," he said.

"In other circumstances I would dispute that remark."

"Really? Well, when I signed up for this detective malarkey I didn't realise my life expectancy would halve overnight, H. You seem to have a talent for upsetting the wrong people."

"*Wrong* people?"

"People with guns, bombs and high explosives."

"Ah yes, *those* wrong people. Well, wrong they may be, but how I could have upset them, heaven only knows."

"Maybe just by *being yourself*," said Mike. "Perhaps you should try acting like someone else."

"Look, I'm not ready for *another* identity change yet, thanks, Mike. Let's get back to business. Someone just tried to kill me. Is there any sign of who might have done it?"

"No, not really. Anonymous parcel from a courier company. Mind you, the delivery guy disappeared sharpish, didn't he? Perhaps he was in on it."

They headed for the park to clear their heads and become less of a sitting target. "You know, Mike, I think I'm beginning to see light at the end of this very long tunnel."

"Go on, inspire me. I've had enough of people trying to

kill me and not getting paid, I might just as well go back to being a doorman. At least there you could see it coming and the money was all right."

"Okay, cards on the table time, Mike. It looks like we have two cases: the golden pig or Scarlatti case, and the Hunting-Baddeley or Summer Lightning case."

"*Had*, I think you'll find," said Mike. "The first client's dead, and in the second case the racehorse is missing in action."

"No, that's where you're wrong," said Hymie.

"Okay, mate, so you're disputing what exactly? The client's death or whether the racehorse is missing? Please tell, and please try to make it convincing, H."

"Well, obviously Lucy Scarlatti is dead and the racehorse seems to be missing, but what I meant was what if the two cases were in fact linked? What if Steffie Scarlatti was involved in both? We're almost certain she killed her sister so she could keep the golden pig, right? We also know from first-hand experience that the Triad is also after that pig, so what if it was the Triad that freed Scarlatti en route to Holloway?"

"Perfectly possible, Hymie, but how does that connect her with the horsenapping?"

"I know it's a bit tenuous, Mike, but I just have this hunch."

"Around your front? It's just a gut, mate."

"Ho ho, there goes another rib," scowled Hymie. "Look, I can't help it if I can't quite explain *why* I think it, but we know the Chinese are heavy gamblers and would therefore follow the racing calendar. We know they wanted to get hold of Scarlatti to find out what happened to the pig, and we know she also enjoys the high life. So if she's still alive, which I for one don't doubt, then there's every chance she might be mixed up in this too."

"No, that's a load of garbage, H. You should go back to being an electrician."

"Oh well, your theory then, brains?"

Arriving at the park they sat on Hymie's regular bench.

"On the downside, we've just lost another case, we've been evicted from the office, we're about to be sued for losing a championship racehorse, we're broke, various people are trying to kill us," said Mike.

"And Benny Baker's just emigrated to Australia," added Hymie.

"And on the upside?"

"Well, you wanted to take charge, where *is* the upside, Mike?"

"Errr, well, we're alive and we've just had a great breakfast at the Black Kat."

"Brilliant. Welcome to the Hymie Goldman school of positive thinking."

"Does it work for you?"

"No, but the alternative doesn't bear thinking about."

"Okay, H, I give in, where *do* we go from here?"

"There's only one place we can possibly go to now," said Hymie.

"Which is?"

"Cheltenham. To the Gold Cup, in fact. Sell anything and everything you can get hold of, Mike. Sell what's left of Ancient Rome, sell your granny if needs be, but we must be at that race; it's the key to everything. Summer Lightning was due to race in it, so whoever stole him is sure to be there. They'll be expecting us." Hymie had never been more certain of anything.

"Well, I fancy a day at the races, H. We may as well go out with a bang as with a whimper."

Part Thirty-Five

March 20th. Cheltenham. Sunrise. Aching limbs, sleep-flecked eyes. Yawn and stretch the waiting away. Threat of something in the air. A horse race. Murder. Money. Corruption and greed. Dewy down on the Cotswold Hills. Ages of irreproachable propriety smug in the promenade, Regency façades, splendour and charm. A minute in the lives of two; two unknown, unsung, unsavoury pieces of trash floating on the ebb tide of the Gold Cup flow.

Brothers and sisters of Eire, and Kentucky, awash with the liquor of the moment, smother the trackside. Breathing smoke through the Arkle haze, damning the weather, the form, odds and days long since gone. For now, for *this* hour the moment is all. Litter patrols, permits, stalls, hoardings, course inspections: myriad lines on some grand autocue. Gates, railings, cars, buses, planes roaring, noise soaring, spiralling, sparks electricity. Voices like a thousand million wheeling gulls. Eyes; smiling, laughing, crying, weighing, watching. Arms waving in a sea of motion. Clamour, tension, built to a point of deception. To be there. Ah, to be there is all. Let them come. Up in the stand, the view commanding for that blur of thundering brightness a silence of awe. Flash red, flash gold, green, blue, yellow, magenta like buzzing flies impatient to meet their end. To cover time and space in a thought. To fly across the heavy turf, light as a feather poised on a knife-edge of terror.

In the throng Goldman like a flea. Hunter and hunted. Empty. Nothing. Free. Itch for his anger. Mock at those last vestiges of pride. Plumbed like the last dregs of curiosity. Were there not moments of lucidity? When the horse was drugged? When the trap was sprung? When his chance came for liberty?

Mike shook his partner by the collar.

"Hymie, Hymie, did we find our answers?"

"…not untwist these last strands of man in me or, most weary, cry I can no more. I can; can something, hope, wish day come, not choose not to be."

"I thought not."

The man mountain carried his seemingly deranged partner out of Prestbury Park.

In the distance an ambulance ferried away two injured spectators with bullet wounds while a police van removed a livid-looking Alfred Jervis. His telescopic umbrella had a forty-five-degree bend in the barrel and he was cursing the arresting officers as they bundled him into the back of the van. Mrs Timmins would never trust him again – Goldman was still alive.

Decca scratched his head. His scalp was itching and he'd noticed that of late it only itched when the name Goldman was mentioned.

"So, let's get this straight, Reidy, you're telling me that there's been a shoot-out at Cheltenham Racecourse on the very day of the Gold Cup?"

"That's right, sir."

"...and that two suspicious-looking men were observed leaving the grounds? A short, shabbily dressed, overweight individual and his outsized accomplice."

"Yes, that's what I was told, Chief."

"It sounds like Goldman and Murphy. Why the sudden interest in horseracing though, eh?"

"We can't be sure it was them, sir."

"I'm sure, Reidy; as sure as ever I can be," said Inspector Decca.

"Well, shouldn't we bring them in for questioning, sir?"

"No, that won't be necessary, thanks, Reidy. Just because they were there, doesn't mean they were actually responsible for the shootings. You know what they tell you at Hendon: know your enemy. Well I know Goldman, like the back of my hand, and I have serious doubts that he can even tie his own shoelaces unaided, let alone shoot someone. Let's just sit back and watch what he's up to. There's precious little left for him to do now," said Decca.

"I don't follow you, Chief."

"Goldman is a dead man, Reidy, a walking, talking, eating, breathing dead man, it's true, but a dead man nevertheless. His time, if he ever had one, is all but over. His business is a failure, half the criminal underworld seems to want to bury him, and he doesn't even have an office to hide in any longer. Mind you, he'd be a real sitting duck if he did. The sad thing is, he still thinks he's on the side of the angels, that he can keep ducking and diving, wheeling and dealing and come up smelling of roses. You know, he still thinks he's a ruddy private detective!"

"I see, sir," said Reidy, who didn't see at all.

"Okay, Reidy, get me a crime report on everything that

happened at Cheltenham today. Leave it in my in-tray. In the meantime, get me Hu."

"Who, sir?" asked Reidy, confused.

"Eddie."

"Eddie who?"

"Exactly."

"Well, sir, if *you* don't know, I'll be blowed if I do," said Reidy, even more confused.

"No, not 'who', 'Hu'. From Hong Kong. The Chinese detective."

"I'm sorry, sir, I've not long come out of hospital, I'm afraid I can't follow you. You'll have to give me his name."

"Listen, Reidy, Hu's a Chinaman, right."

"Bruce Lee's the only one that springs to mind, sir."

Inspector Decca stared morosely into the middle distance, while his brain replayed the conversation he had just been having with his junior officer.

"Look, get lost, Reidy, go and do some work. Send Potter to see me, will you…"

Looking peeved and confused, Reidy turned and left the office.

Part Thirty-Six

The ancient and inscrutable face of the oriental fixer Master Lau appeared drawn and irritated. He hated playing draughts, especially to lose, but he had to be civil to the old bat, at least for now.

"Well played, Mrs Timmins, you are most accomplished at the art of draughts."

"All games are alike to me, Lau. I play to win or not at all. I gather the Gold Cup proved profitable?"

"Certainly, madam, certainly. We made a very satisfactory return on our investment."

"Very gratifying. Was it enough to settle your outstanding debt to the Baron?"

"Of course. Will a cheque be acceptable?"

"I should think so, yes. You have never been known to default."

"No, madam, there can be no life without honour," said Lau, arrogantly.

"I'm glad to hear you say it. Which brings me to the small matter of Hymie Goldman. I understand he is *still* alive. What went wrong this time?!"

"It grieves me to say it, madam, but you must take some of the responsibility for that particular oversight yourself."

"How so, Lau?" asked Edna Timmins.

"Your own agent as they say 'queered our pitch'."

"My agent?"

"Please, madam, give me credit for some intelligence. Your agent, Alfred Jervis – or Harry the Hit, as he is known in Teddington – was arrested by the police after bungling his attempts to kill Goldman.

"I had an agent at the trackside who would have made sure of the job in the ordinary course of events."

"What, Steffanie Scarlatti?"

"Madam, I cannot be expected to disclose the identities or methods of my agents. It is in your own interests as well as my own. What you do not know can not be imputed to you."

"I know very well you were using Scarlatti on the job."

"As you wish. I have no desire to get into a dispute over who was responsible when I know the answer very well."

"You forced my hand by your slackness in completing our contract," snapped Mrs Timmins.

"Madam, you insult me. Would you like me to refund the money you paid on the contract or should I complete it?" He didn't care anymore, he just wanted an end to her petty recriminations.

"I will give you twenty-four hours, Lau. Kill Goldman, or give me my money back and I will make my own arrangements. Of course, if you fail, your reputation will suffer."

"I think not, madam. Perhaps before Cheltenham, but

now you have taken direct action, my reputation is safe enough. Are you sure you wouldn't prefer your money back? In the scheme of things Goldman's life is such a small matter."

"Small matter?! The man is a curse. He must die, don't you understand?! Were it not for his incompetence, Tiddles would still be alive today. I cannot rest easy in my own mind until the world is rid of him!" She had clearly lost the plot where Goldman was concerned.

Scarlatti would see to it, thought Lau. It just seemed a little pointless, not to mention beneath him, having a hopeless idiot put to death just to placate a vindictive old woman.

"When do I get the money for the drugs contract, Lau?" Mrs Timmins was nothing if not greedy.

"I will send it over by courier tomorrow," he said. "On reflection, I will send you the cash. It cuts down on the laundering, you know." He smiled the smile of the dyspeptic. He was imagining the look on her face when she found Steffanie Scarlatti on her doorstep.

"Be sure you do. I expect he will also be able to give me an update on Goldman."

"Certainly, madam. Goodbye," said Lau, with a tight-lipped smile.

As he sat in his pink velour armchair later that evening, enjoying his cocoa over an excellent new game show, *Loadsa Loot*, he was disturbed by a sharp rapping on the window. What made it stranger still was the fact that he lived on the fourth floor.

"Who's there?" he asked, not unnaturally.

He was answered by silence.

Perhaps it was a pigeon flying into the window. No, pigeons didn't knock. He lifted the sash window and peered out into the deepening gloom. The traffic's hum floated into the room. Outside it was beginning to drizzle and clouds were gathering over the darkening streets.

"London," he thought. "Who needs it?!"

A pigeon, which had been roosting on the grimy ledge of a neighbouring building, struck its wings in flight, shattering his drifting calm and causing him to straighten up abruptly.

His movement was checked as the feline fingers of a black-gloved hand closed tightly on his throat and pulled his head down to the sill. In a flash of animal grace she was upon him, springing through the casement into the room and kicking Lau to the ground with a powerful swipe of her right boot.

He lurched across the room, still gasping for air from his recent partial asphyxiation, barely managing to compose himself in time to meet her next assault. She slid her hunting knife from its scabbard on her belt and lunged at his chest in a vicious attack, her bloodcurdling scream of rage simultaneously ripping through the evening's stillness.

He desperately prepared himself to defend and counter-attack. With the poise and grace earned in a lifetime's martial arts practice, Lau sidestepped the wild assault and followed through with a power punch to the ribs. She was fast, but not *that* fast. He caught her on the third rib and she careened into the corner of the hardwood dining table, inflicting both damage and injury to herself as she fell.

Lau unsheathed a 500-year-old ceremonial samurai sword from pride of place on the wall above the mantelpiece and leapt forward with cat-like tread to finish the job.

"This is to avenge Chiu Mann," he cried, as he raised the sword's finely honed blade above his head to deliver the *coup de grâce*.

Like Chiu Mann he had written off his assailant too quickly. She rolled sideways out of the path of bloody demise and pulled a small derringer pistol from the back of her left boot.

"It's time for you to pay, Lau. Pay with your life, of course," she sneered.

It was her turn to underestimate her adversary, to understand at last that he was not called *Master* Lau for nothing.

He appeared to twist a small packet of crystals concealed in his sleeve and then he simply disappeared into a purple haze. The smoke billowed out of his robe, filling the room in an all-pervading mist at frenetic speed.

Steffanie Scarlatti was not about to be denied her triumph, nor her revenge so easily. Raising the pistol to shoulder height, she blasted away at the space where Lau's last seen corporeal form had been until she had completely discharged the weapon.

The mist cleared. Lau's cape appeared to be suspended in mid-air before her, torn in several places by bullet holes, singed by the passage of gunpowder and wet with something that looked like blood. The cloak fell to the ground and Lau reappeared in a new silk-trimmed gown, seemingly uninjured. He lifted his wooden walking stick and smacked it hard across Scarlatti's head.

"OOF! AARGH!" she spluttered.

"Never forget I am your master. It shall always be so while you owe me a debt of honour."

"I owe you nothing, Lau, nothing. You cannot steal my freedom with your cheap tricks and your old words."

"You are bound to me like a slave to its master. Until you have completed our bargain you belong to me, body and soul. You will never be free until you have fulfilled your promise," he insisted.

She hated to admit it to herself, but she *was* scared of him. He didn't play by her rules, or any rules that she could fathom, and that made him unpredictable and dangerous.

"You have sworn to kill Edna Timmins and Hymie Goldman, as the price of your freedom. Make no mistake, I gave you your freedom and I can as easily take it away again, but I am a reasonable man. Goldman means nothing to me. By my faith the idiot is sacred so I shall reprieve him. However, in lieu of sparing you this chore I ask only that you take this briefcase to Mrs Timmins, kill her and return the case to me."

"Why take the case at all, simply to return it?"

"If you fail to arrive with the case, you will never meet Mrs Timmins," he said cryptically.

"I see." She could see that the contents of the case were worth something.

"Goodbye, Scarlatti, and good luck with your mission," he said.

"We make our own luck, Lau."

"Not always."

Outside in the doorway of a shop stood a man in a trench coat, muffled against the cold and rain. He had been standing there for several hours already, but seemed unmoved by the weather and the monotony of his wait.

Scarlatti appeared at the ground-floor entrance to the building facing his vantage point, and he cautiously prepared to follow her. She seemed to pause at the sight of the torrential downpour and re-entered the building.

Mike crossed the street and carefully followed her at a distance as she crossed the foyer. He watched her enter the lift and clocked the indicator as it moved to the first floor before stopping, then he raced up the building's backstairs to the first floor, just in time to see Scarlatti's back disappearing into one of the apartments. He knocked on the door.

She eyed it suspiciously. Who could know she was here? Was she being paranoid? Better safe than sorry.

"Come in," she said.

The door flew open to reveal Murphy, blotting out the light from the corridor.

"Hello, Steffie."

"Murphy? What are you doing here?"

"I've come about the golden pig."

"I don't know what you're talking about. Are you delusional or something?" Who did he think he was, this *doorman?*

As she looked at him it crossed her mind that it would be difficult to miss him from where she was standing. It would be difficult to miss a target that big, period.

As if to answer the expression in her eyes he removed his old service revolver from his trench-coat pocket and pointed it at her.

"Don't start any funny business, Steffie, I just want the pig."

Did she play dumb, or come clean? If she came clean it would probably mean killing him, but he'd started it. There was nothing childish about her, at least not on the glossy, hard-boiled surface.

She opened the top drawer of a filing cabinet, removed a tatty plastic bag from the back and took out the golden statuette he had heard so much about.

"Is this what you wanted?" she asked him.

"Yes, although I hadn't expected it to be so small."

"Small is beautiful, Murphy, though I wouldn't expect *you* to understand. Of course, the rule only holds good for *objets d'art*." She smiled at him.

He could feel all his distrust and contempt for her melting away, yet he knew deep down inside that to let down his guard could prove fatal. There were many men who could testify to that.

"Put it back in the bag and give it to me," he told her.

"I'm intrigued to know on what basis you stake your claim, Murphy. Is it just by force of arms?"

"If it's any of your business, I'm a partner in JP Confidential and this statuette belongs to one of our clients."

She laughed hysterically.

"You and Goldman? That's a hoot. You call yourselves a private investigations bureau?!"

It wasn't the reaction he had been expecting, but it made it easier to keep his hatred alive. Yet it also made him angry that what had begun as a source of pride should have degenerated into something farcical. He *was* a partner, and he was here because he knew Hymie would stand no chance. She had fooled him into thinking she was a seventeen-year-old trainee for six months. Next time it could prove fatal for the poor sap.

"Just do as I say," he barked.

"Or what, you're going to shoot me? I can't see it, Murphy. You may be a dab hand at beating up tough nuts outside a club, but you won't kill a woman in cold blood." Her gambling instincts came to the fore.

"Try me," he said, coldly.

He wouldn't kill her, he knew that, but he was certainly willing to shoot her, if it meant he could get out of there alive.

"Pass me the bag, now!"

She started folding up the bag, but just as she seemed about to pass it over, she threw it at his head and dived for cover behind the settee.

He knew he may not get another chance.

BLAM! BLAM! CLICK...

She screamed in pain as she hit the carpet and clutched at her left shoulder, which seemed to be on fire. A searing pain was throbbing all down her left arm. He had actually shot her. She removed her derringer from its holster and trained it at chest height at the space above the settee, waiting to blow him away. Mike meanwhile was struggling with concussion. The golden pig had caught the side of his head and he was feeling decidedly groggy. He knew he had to get out of there, knew that the odds were turning against him and wondered if his gun was empty or if it was just the third chamber.

Lifting the pig in the plastic bag Murphy retreated down the corridor. He knew he wouldn't have time for the lift so started to run to the staircase. The realisation suddenly dawned on Steffanie Scarlatti that she was no longer the quarry but the hunter, and she reached the corridor just as Murphy was entering the stairwell. She ran after him, pulled open the door to the stairwell and fired down the staircase at him.

BLAM! BLAM! BLAM!

The bullets ricocheted off the staircase and their thunderous clamour echoed through the chamber.

"AARGH!"

He was hit. A momentary pause and then he kept moving. His only chance lay in flight. When she reached the bottom of the stairwell, he was gone, though an occasional trail of bloodspots marked his passing.

"An injured animal is a dangerous one," she thought.

She should know. She returned to her apartment and

removed her jacket to examine the wound. She had been lucky, she supposed; it was no more than a flesh wound. No bones seemed to be broken, and although it hurt like hell, it wasn't going to hold her back for long. She'd need a good plastic surgeon, of course, or she wouldn't be wearing any more topless dresses at Cannes.

Murphy would keep. Yes, he had the golden pig, but he was injured, maybe even dying. If she kept her appointment with Edna Timmins, it would give him time to check into a hospital or bleed to death. Either way, he would soon be dead and the pig would be back where it belonged.

She dressed her wound with difficulty, but needed to staunch the blood and maintain the image of composure and professionalism for the old bat. Once Timmins was dead she could see to Murphy and disappear somewhere warm with the golden pig and the contents of Lau's briefcase.

It was time to check out of this open prison.

Part Thirty-Seven

Hymie was becoming a connoisseur of hospitals, NHS ones at least. Like a train spotter collecting numbers he had started to keep a tally of which hospitals he had visited, perhaps with a view to one day publishing the definitive consumer guide. Not that anyone would want to read it, of course – it was all most people could do to avoid the ruddy places.

He lay comatose in yet another hospital bed, in Edgware General.

A nurse paused outside the curtain wall, looked inside briefly at the battered man of fortune, and resumed her journey.

"What's the matter with him, Doctor?"

"Nervous exhaustion, lack of sleep, too much fast food, caffeine and sugar in his diet...I could go on, but it would only bore you. Why don't I buy you lunch instead? Or better still, dinner?"

"You'll be lucky to get out of here for long enough to eat dinner, Simon," said the nurse, roguishly.

"Too true," he said, forlornly.

"They seemed to think he might have been taking drugs when they brought him in, had he?" asked the nurse.

"No. Well, not in the last forty-eight hours anyway."

In the alternative reality in Hymie's head a message was coming through from the great beyond.

"Hymie!"

No response.

"HYMIE!!" A voice like thunder.

The voice grew and grew until it filled his head, like the continuous deafening peal of ancient church bells.

"Yes, God. How can I help you?"

He was floating on the ceiling of the ward, looking down at himself in bed. His bruised and battered body looked old and tired, but somehow smaller than it seemed from the inside. His mind, his spirit, his soul were all alive and kicking, but that poor old body needed a rest.

"Just a social visit. You've been overdoing it, that's all."

"Can I have it in writing?"

"What do you think? I just thought I'd come and tell you that the end is nearly in sight."

"I'm not going to die, am I?"

"No, not just yet. Well, you've got a business to run, haven't you?"

"That's right, I have. I've got a business partner now as well, you know."

"Yes, a good man. Murphy, isn't it?" asked God.

"You know very well it is."

"I suppose I do," agreed God, modestly.

"Have I still got to fight the champion of evil?"

"Not today, no. You'd be amazed how often evil simply destroys itself. Still, it pays to be ready. Never go down without a fight. Always be the best you can. You know the rules. You even try to live by them in your own strange way. Good luck," said God, departing.

"Thanks, God."

He was awake at last in his hospital bed. Alone and tired, but somehow contented, he had been granted the gift of God's peace.

Part Thirty-Eight

"Take a seat, Lieutenant Hu."

"Please, call me Eddie, I'm not on duty now."

"Oh, right. Well, you can call me Ray then. Thanks for sparing me some of your time on leave. We've been making good progress with the Triad investigation, but we can't put names to all the faces and I thought you were probably one of the only guys who could help us," said Decca.

"As I said before, Inspect..."

"Ray."

"Right, as I said, Ray, I'd be more than happy to help. My files are in the bureau's offices in Hong Kong, but I can probably identify most of the operators from memory."

"Good. Now here's an interesting-looking character – any idea who he is?"

"As it happens, yes. That, Ray, is Lau – Master Lau, they call him. We believe he is either in charge of one of the London-based Triads or is at the very least one of their senior generals. Yet, despite that, we have nothing on him. He's at least sixty years old, has short grey hair and dresses like an old school Chinese mandarin. You probably think he looks like Fu Manchu, right?"

"Funny you should say that, Eddie."

"Well, I'm afraid there's nothing funny about him. He's a fearsome organiser of all things illegal, and a ruthless killer, responsible for some of the bloodiest gangland murders of the past decade. He is also highly skilled at distancing himself from the sordid end of Triad operations."

"Do you know anything else about him? Known addresses, contacts, hobbies?"

"Very little. He seems to be almost untouchable. He

probably has more aliases than anyone living. The little we do know came from an agent of one of the main drug pushers in Hong Kong. He was found knifed on the *Star* ferry leaving Kowloon just a few days later," said Eddie Hu.

"Do you have anything on his activities in the UK?" asked Decca.

"No, that's outside my jurisdiction I'm afraid. You can probably tell me about what he's been up to here."

"He was seen at a major crime scene on Beachy Head a couple of months ago, but no one knew who he was, so when he disappeared we had no way of tracing him. He was mentioned in one of the witness statements though. Some guy called Goldman claimed to have been kidnapped by him."

"Lucky for him you got there when you did."

"Try telling him that, Eddie!" said Decca.

"Goldman claimed that this Master Lau character was after a golden statuette of a pig and that he would do anything to recover it."

"Not the golden pig of Wei Ling?!" speculated Hu, with wild enthusiasm.

"You know something about it?" asked Decca.

"If it's the statuette I'm thinking of, no one has seen it for years. It's a solid gold temple ornament. Word had it that one of the most violent drug barons had struck a deal for it and the buyer had reneged."

"I didn't credit the story much at the time. Goldman was always an habitual liar," explained Decca.

"Who is this Goldman, and where is he now?" asked Eddie Hu.

"Oh, he usually shows up in one hospital or another if you wait around long enough. He's a walking disaster area – a no-account private investigator, blessed with unfeasible luck. I sometimes think he must have as many lives as a cat, it's just a shame the same can't be said for those associating with him, who usually come to a sticky end, poor devils."

"Well, it sounds like Goldman could use some protection if he knows anything about Master Lau," continued Hu.

"I guess you're right. I'll get Terse onto it straightaway. Thanks for your help, Eddie, enjoy your vacation."

"Thanks, Ray, perhaps our paths will cross again some day."

"Count on it."

Part Thirty-Nine

The discreet ring of the doorbell chimed in another overpriced West London apartment.

"That will be the courier with my briefcase, let him in," said Edna Timmins to the domestic staff.

One of the doormen lifted the latch and allowed the security chain to play out to its fullest extent.

"What's the password?" he asked.

"Summer Lightning," she purred.

The door swung open to reveal that fleshly panorama of earthly paradise for men, Steffanie Scarlatti. Until she killed you, like the Black Widow spider she so closely resembled, you would think yourself in heaven in her embrace or basking in the sunshine of her smile.

They were momentarily stunned. Things can happen in a moment: bad things.

BLAM! BLAM!

Two heavy bodies slumped to the floor, still smiling as they died.

She lowered her pistol and stepped over the redundant doormen.

"I was wondering whether Lau would send you. I didn't think he would trust you, but I can be wrong. It happens to the best of us," said Mrs Timmins.

Scarlatti leapt back in surprise. Edna Timmins was nothing if not a cool customer in a hot spot. She smiled a relaxed smile and undid the safety catch on her pistol.

"I assure you, Miss Scarlatti, I rarely shoot at people, but never miss."

"It's Ms," hissed Scarlatti.

"Are you married?"

"Don't be absurd."

"Then it's *Miss*. I don't know *what* they teach young people today, but it isn't English."

They stood facing each other across the reception hall like two wildcats spoiling for a fight, but the older cat, with the wisdom of age and experience on her side, was leaving nothing to chance.

"Don't make any sudden moves, Miss Scarlatti, I would be only too happy to shoot you. You are without a doubt the most arrogant and annoying young person I have met in many a year."

"You say the sweetest things."

Mrs Timmins began to frown, but then something occurred to her and she regained her equanimity.

"Come and sit down, Miss Scarlatti, but let me take your gun first, if you please, we don't want any more accidents."

Scarlatti dropped her gun on the parquet flooring with a dull thud.

"Did Lau ask you to shoot my doormen or was that your own idea?"

"They were a threat," she snarled.

"What to? World peace? The ozone layer? I'm afraid you're not making very much sense. It's clear to me that you hold other peoples' lives cheap, and I deplore your callousness."

She poured out two cups of tea from a fine white bone-china teapot.

Steffanie Scarlatti stared incredulously at the old lady. Could this really be the face of the ruthless gangland boss she had heard such terrible tales about? She doubted it. She probably ran her crime empire through her lieutenants – psychopathic lunatics with a mother fixation to a man. And yet...who would have imagined herself to be a vicious killer?

A flash of suppressed rage played about the lines on the old woman's face like an electric current flickering around a circuit. It wouldn't take very much to provoke her to anger, and then what? Was she capable of murder? In the final analysis we all were, surely, thought Scarlatti.

"I'd like to play a little game now, dear," said Mrs Timmins.

"I don't play games."

"How sad, but you'll enjoy this one, I promise. I call it Serbian roulette, it's like Russian roulette only a little more one-sided."

"What are you babbling about, you silly old woman!"

The lines around Timmins' eyes and mouth registered her annoyance, but she remained mistress of her tongue.

"You don't imagine I would give you a gun for even one second, surely?"

There was only one strategy left to her. She must goad the old woman into making a mistake – truly a dangerous game.

"No, even *you* couldn't be that stupid," said Scarlatti.

"As I was saying, I do so miss a good game of Serbian roulette. No one will play with me anymore. They say I cheat."

"And do you?"

"Oh yes, shamelessly," confided Edna Timmins. "The aim of the game is simply to answer three questions correctly."

"Supposing I do?"

"You go home in a taxi."

"And if I don't?"

"You go home in a hearse."

"Ah, one of *those* games," said Scarlatti.

"*Those* games?"

"Strictly for suckers!"

"No matter, I only thought to give you a sporting chance. If you really don't want it I may as well just shoot you now," added Edna T.

"Now I come to think of it, I must have been confusing it with some other game," said Scarlatti.

"I'm so glad."

She was insane – completely, comprehensively raving mad. It took one to know one.

"May I have one last request, before we play your game? It's traditional, you know, before a big match."

"It depends," said Timmins.

"On what?"

"On the request. I would hate to see you get an unfair advantage over me."

"Nothing could be further from my thoughts, Mrs Timmins. I simply wanted to see what was in the briefcase. I assumed it was either cash or drugs."

"Cash in fact: £2,000,000 in hard currency. I approve – you are a woman after my own heart. It is a great pity you have to die, but there it is. I would offer you a job if I could, but you're far too dangerous. It gets very tiresome continuously having to watch one's back at my age." Edna Timmins lifted the briefcase and placed it squarely in her visitor's lap.

"Treat yourself, my dear," she said.

Scarlatti had been looking for something to throw at her hostess but became genuinely curious to see £2,000,000 in banknotes. She pressed open the dual combination locks at the top of the case and flipped open the lid. She barely had time to notice that the case was full of scrap paper before the movement of the locks triggered the trembler device concealed in the case and the room was engulfed in a fireball.

Their screaming lasted no more than a few short minutes, and there was no one to mourn their passing. Within an hour the apartment was reduced to a gutted shell.

A few streets away, at the Oaktree Veterinary Surgery, Cedric was enjoying a nice bit of cuttlefish to recuperate after a particularly challenging beak trim, blithely unaware that he was now an orphan.

Part Forty

They sat in their adjacent offices at 792A Finchley Road reading the papers. Hymie, as befitted a man newly enriched by a large insurance payout, was reading the *Financial Times* and finding it hard going. Apart from providing a use for the world's reserves of pink paper, what did any of it *mean*? He turned to the sports section and did a double-take. There *was* some justice in the world after all, he sighed. The Hunting-Baddeley yard had been prosecuted for race-fixing. "Let Lady Muck laugh that one off!" he smiled to himself. Lightning had been found safe and well behind a false wall in the stable block.

The Total Disaster Insurance Corporation, or Total DIC as Hymie referred to them, had proved very appreciative of not having to shell out £2,000,000 for a golden statue of a pig that most people wouldn't have given shelf space to. At last JP Confidential had a bright and solvent future.

Mike, who seemed to be reading the *Finchley News*, was secretly reading *Classics from the Comics*, which he had inserted inside the paper to maintain the illusion that he took an interest in the wider world. He hadn't quite mastered the partner's art of not giving a hoot what the staff thought of his behaviour, however eccentric.

Outside his office, Janey Johnson, the new office junior-cum-receptionist was busy cutting out newspaper articles relating to the firm's celebrated recovery of the stolen artefact known as the golden pig. They would be dining out on it for years.

Suddenly Mike's attention was drawn to an article in the news on the discovery of two women's bodies in a burnt-out Kensington flat. The police were looking into it, inevitably. Mike had been over his final shoot-out with Steffie Scarlatti again and again in his mind, and was now more certain than ever that he was lucky to be alive. Only his bullet-proof vest had saved him. He would keep it on forever, he decided, though not in the shower, obviously. It looked as though she was finally dead, though the police weren't confirming anything until they had checked her dental records.

The buzzer on the intercom sounded outside their offices.

"Your nine-thirty is here, Mr Goldman," called Janey.

"Send her in, please," said Hymie.

This time she would see sense. Half a million quid for a business *this* good? It was preposterous! With a high profile and successful case behind them surely the sky was the limit for JP Confidential. He could see it now – branches in every city, a call centre in Bradford and a string of Rolls-Royces, platinum credit cards and glamorous assistants.

"Hello again, Mr Goldman," said Sarah Chandar. "You're a difficult man to track down."

"I'm sorry, Sarah, I've been working deep undercover. So far undercover I thought I might never get out again."

"And now I know why. Congratulations on another successful case. Are you ready to talk terms on the sale of the business?"

"Of course, that's what you're here for."

"Good. Now, Mr Goldman, or should I call you Hymie?"

He nodded.

"I've taken the liberty of drafting an outline agreement, for your approval."

He flipped over the pages and frowned. "But the price is only £500,000, Sarah, surely the business is worth more than that? With our new profile in the industry we ought to be looking for £1,000,000," he added.

"Not without a lot more investment, Hymie. There are only three members of staff and twenty-four hours in a day, after all. I represent Ceefer Capital, not the National Lottery."

Hymie tapped on the window for Mike to join them, and he entered the room.

"Mike, this is Sarah Chandar from Ceefer Capital. She's made an offer to buy the business."

Mike's face fell.

"Don't you want to know how much they've offered, and what your share is?" asked Hymie, surprised at his reaction.

"No, Hymie, because you'd be making a terrible mistake, mate. This is our *livelihood*. If you sell that then you become redundant. Oh, you can live on the money while it lasts, but money isn't everything. You know, nowadays I get up in the morning looking forward to working at JP Confidential. I'm a partner in the firm so I don't have to take any crap from anyone and I know that what I do makes a difference. I care about this firm, Hymie! If we worked for some big multinational corporation, all that would change. I might as well be a doorman at the Rainbow Rooms again, because whatever they offered me, I'd still be a wage slave. I'm surprised you can't see it yourself. Think of all the years you've struggled to get to where you are, and for what? To give it away to the first venture capitalist that comes along? They're not running a charity, you know!"

Hymie became quiet and contemplative, while Sarah Chandar opened her mouth to speak, but stopped herself. This was *their* decision. It was a setback, of course, but there would always be another chance, people were basically greedy.

Mike smiled at Hymie and shrugged. "It was good while it lasted," he said, resigned to his fate. Hymie smiled back. He had looked forward to this moment for so long but he had forgotten what was important.

"I'm afraid the deal's off, Sarah," he said. "Mike's right, we can't sell the business, it's all we have. It's kept me going for the last few years, when otherwise I would have thrown in the towel." Tears began to well up in his eyes, so he blew his nose quickly and surreptitiously wiped them away.

"I understand," said Sarah, and left them.

Later, Hymie began to doubt whether he had done the right thing, but Mike was steadfast and the business couldn't function any longer without him. Instead of an ending, the meeting became a new beginning for the two detectives. Cases would increasingly find *them*; good cases, providing interesting work and rich rewards. For now, all that lay in the future, and the future, as they said of the past, was another country.